It Had To Be You

The Rose Prairie Series
SIERRA SHIPLEY

Table of Contents

Books By Sierra

The Claiming Her Series
His Temptation
His Disaster
His Reward
His Challenge

The Rose Prairie Series
All Tangled Up
Tied In Nots
It Had To Be You

Interconnected Stand Alone
Yes, Captain
Hey, Neighbor

The Single Dads Club
Loved by the Single Dad
Nanny for the Single Dad
Desired by the Single Dad

Prologue

Smith

"Anyone else have any *other* ideas?" Mr. Shannon poses the question for what has to be the tenth time this meeting. Monday meetings are full of discussions about future articles and he's shot down every idea thrown out. Looking around the conference room, everyone's already scraping the bottom of the barrel.

The Daily Click is a fast-growing online newspaper and Mr. Shannon is hell-bent on finding a human interest story that's never been done before.

My pen taps against my notebook, the soft thud mingling with the other anxious ticks made by the journalists around me. Chairs swivel and someone coughs lightly, no one daring to make eye contact with our boss. Not that we're scared of him, we're just out of ideas.

"I think I have something." A small hand raises in the air, the young intern wide-eyed. She cautiously stands as all eyes shift to her seat in the corner next to the coffeemaker. "Um, well." She stammers clearing her throat, her hands clasping nervously in front of her. "This last Christmas my friends and I went to this small town — like really small. We'd heard that they have this event on Christmas Eve, so we decided to check it out. It's normally only a Christmas thing, but I guess the girl they hired throws all these seasonal events drawing huge

3

crowds. My friends have even been talking about going to their Fall Festival."

The silence in the room hangs heavy, all eyes shifting to Mr. Shannon. The older man scrapes his hand along his chin, his lips puckered in thought. "How'd you hear about it?"

"That's the thing. We can't remember." She shrugs her shoulders. "I guess they've been doing it for like forever and hotels in the area have started selling out every time they put on another event."

"What's the name of this place?"

She looks down at her feet in thought. "Rose something." Her eyes flutter shut, her face scrunching as she tries to remember. "Prairie!" She announces loudly. "It's called Rose Prairie. It's about a three-hour drive from here. Their fall festival starts this Friday." She pulls out her phone, her thumbs quickly typing until she finds what she's looking for. With a satisfied smile, she holds her phone up to show the online flyer.

It's simple. Fall leaves and pumpkins decorate the edges with large black letters. *"Join us for our first annual Fall Festival. Come see what Rose Prairie is all about!"*

Something about that name sounds familiar. Although I have no idea where this place is, awareness prickles at the back of my neck like a forgotten memory, no matter how hard you think of it, it never comes back.

"I'm intrigued." Mr. Shannon murmurs, his large fists settling on the polished conference table. "Matt." All eyes shift to me, my pen stopping its motion. "I want you to go to this Rose Prairie. Get in touch with the person who puts on all of these events. Learn about the town, its culture, and how these events help the town. I want you there for their festival. I expect to have the article on my desk the next day."

A strand of my black hair bounces on my forehead as I nod. "Yes, sir."

Looks like I'm heading to Rose Prairie. *Wherever the hell that is.*

Chapter One

Cara

The bell rings as another customer steps into Tall, Dark, and Coffee, adding to the growing line that nearly reaches the door. There must be something in the fall air that has everyone rushing for a warm beverage.

If only they'd bother to buy a book or two, I think bitterly.

Tall, Dark, and Coffee is my baby. My dream. Some kids grew up wanting to be firefighters, teachers, or doctors. But not me. Nope, I wanted to own a bookstore. What goes hand in hand with books better than coffee? There's a reason most chain bookstores have that well-known coffee shop inside. Only now it's more like the coffee is funding my bookstore and not the other way around.

I proudly sell and advertise a wide variety of books, but my main focus is romance. Sure, there are dedicated non-fiction sections and that area of the store that houses the Nicholas Sparks books, but they pale in comparison to the romance selection.

Unfortunately, in this small town, books are not as high of a priority as coffee. This is why I wish there was some way to have people buy more books. I'm lucky if I'm able to sell three books a day, and even that is pushing it.

Order after order is made, and Jessie and I do our best to keep up with them all. We take turns working the register and making the orders, and before long, the morning bustle dies down.

The busiest time of our day happens right around eight o'clock. We open at six for that early bird crowd, but we get flooded with high schoolers stopping in before school, the parents of younger kids getting their pick-me-up after dropping kids off, or the old men on their way out of town for work. There's the mid-morning rush of college students from Rosewood who usually sit at the tables with their books out as they work on assignments.

The chain coffee shop set up on the outskirts of town cut business down, but once the novelty wore off, people came back to their local shop. That's what I love about Rose Prairie. Say what you want about small-town folks, but they are loyal.

After I graduated from Rosewood College, I spent some time in the city learning the ins and outs of managing a business. You know, get that real-world experience. There were many lessons I had to learn in my short time there, and picking the right location was one of them. Honestly, it was the easiest one I learned then.

After spending six months as an intern, I came right back to the town that raised me. Got a small business loan from Mr. Moser who helped me set up my first bank account when I was fifteen. Bought the storefront that sat empty for years since the Halstons retired and never looked back.

It took some time to get things up and running though and I had my fair share of setbacks, but looking around my little corner of the world, I can say I'm happy with what I've accomplished.

Sunlight streams through the windows, and soft music plays through the speakers as regulars enjoy their coffee, and read their newspapers. People chat happily with one another as they wait in line. No one is in a huge rush to get a complicated order in twenty seconds so they can sprint to work.

It's my slice of heaven.

Jessie, Eileen, and I might have gone a little overboard with the fall decorations, but it adds to the store's charm. Auburn, gold, and orange leaf garland twined with fairy lights run down the length of the bookshelves, tiny pumpkins nestled into it. Each small table has a centerpiece made up of a vase with chrysanthemums.

The bell on the door dings as I'm wiping down the counters after our busy morning rush. "Cara, just the woman I was looking for." Sammie plops her bag on the counter and leans in, her cheeks flushed from the cool air. Long dark hair poking out from under her hat that's the same color green as her eyes.

"Mocha?" I ask out of politeness because she hardly orders anything else.

"Yes." She plasters a toothy grin on her face. "I need two to go. Levi needs one too." She taps a finger on the counter. "But also, I have a favor to ask."

Sammie worked for me for a year before she got the job of being the event coordinator. She's been a breath of fresh air for our small town, but she's always busy planning the next event. I swear she's in constant motion at all times.

I roll my eyes in faux exasperation. "What do you need this time?" The loud noise of the milk frother dims her response and I have to ask her to say it again.

"A journalist is coming to town and I need you to show him around." Sammie puts on a too-wide smile.

"Um, why?" Dread sinks into my bones at her request. I know she's not going to ask me for something dramatic, like helping her bury a body, but I don't want to have to tell her no.

She settles herself on the counter, her eyes tracking me as I work. "So I was contacted by this newspaper about doing a human interest story on Rose Prairie. And, well, I'm busy with the Fall Festival. I'll be able to meet with him for a little bit, but I can't be distracted. That's where you come in. I need a true Rosie to showcase the town."

"You know I'm not a '*true Rosie*'." The air quotes I make look awkward around the stainless steel frothing pitcher and I almost drop it. Maybe she'll back down and I'll have avoided this whole favor issue. *Fingers crossed.*

She rolls her eyes, scoffing. "Shut up, yes you are. Plus, you're a business owner with an invested interest in the town." Sammie inches closer over the counter as she watches me pour the steaming milk into her coffee and I can almost see her salivating. She practically groans when I grab the whipped cream.

A Rosie is a born and bred native of Rose Prairie and seeing as I moved here as a pre-teen, a Rosie I am not.

Chocolate sauce dribbles across the whipped cream before I press down the lids. "Why don't you get Lori to show him around?" My last beacon of hope rests upon the most unlikely of shoulders. Lori Haverford knows this town inside and out. It's her greatest passion in life, especially since her husband passed away several years ago. When Sammie was hired as the town's event coordinator to Lori, Sammie was here to destroy everything.

Her face falls, her expression turning serious. "I wouldn't do that to my *worst* enemy. You know Lori Haverford would probably drive the poor man out of town and then we'll never get the publicity we need. We may be mending things, but Lori is a handful on a good day."

Dammit, she's right.

I add coffee sleeves to the warm cups before setting them in front of a waiting Sammie as she slides her payment to me. She bats those large green eyes, pouting out her lower lip as she begs me to say yes.

My hip cocks as I lean into the counter and sigh. I've run out of options. "What's his name?"

Her eyes grow wide and she bounces on her feet. "His name is Mathew, he works at *The Daily Click* and he'll be here tomorrow. I've carved out some time to meet with him later in the morning and into the afternoon, but other than that, he's all yours."

"How long?" Please say it's for one day...

"The rest of the week. Just through Saturday." She rushes her words like saying them faster lessens their impact.

My jaw drops audibly with a small pop. "Sammie," I gasp.

"Just think. It'll be great for business. You can take him around town and show him all the charm Rose Prairie has to offer. Oh, maybe you can get him together with all the small business owners so he can mention them in his article. Levi even said his parents would help if they needed to. I mean, really, there's a lot you can do to keep him occupied." She tosses her bag on her shoulder and grabs the steaming coffee. "Thank you for doing this." The words come out jumbled as she heads to the door. "See you tomorrow," she calls over her shoulder, practically running away before I can make a protest.

What the hell am I supposed to do with a journalist?

Hell, there's hardly anything in Rose Prairie to keep *me* occupied and I freaking live here.

All throughout the workday I think about what in the world I can show this guy. I'm sure he'll be competent enough to explore the town on his own, so I won't have to do much, right? Sammie's suggestion of having him meet with the other business owners isn't a bad idea.

Thanks to Sammie's events, our little town is thriving. What started out as our annual Christmas Spectacular has blossomed into carnivals, festivals, and celebrations. It's exciting. The college gets involved and many students volunteer which has really brought the community together. I guess I can play my part in helping out our town.

Fishing my phone from my apron, I pull up the group thread for all the business owners in the town square. If I'm going to make this happen, I need to get the ball rolling. Just getting everyone to agree on a specific day and time is going to be a nightmare.

Now I understand why Sammie pawned this off on me.

Chapter Two

Smith

"You leaving us, Clark?" The firm pat on my shoulder and the teasing lilt to the voice could only belong to Bruce. He quickly matches my pace as I walk through the lobby.

The Daily Click has been growing in popularity since it first started three years ago, and I love my job. One downside? The staff itself is close-knit and maybe a little *too* comfortable with one another. During my first week in the office, Erin, our office manager, forgot my name—not that I blame her. My friends growing up called me Smith, and it stuck. When Erin couldn't remember, she asked for Clark Kent. Aka, me. I understand the comparison. In the right lighting, I might look like an off-brand Clark. Tall, dark hair, blue eyes, and a dorkish charm help to complete the resemblance. It's worse when I wear my dark-rimmed glasses, which I stopped wearing in the office rather quickly after the nickname stuck.

"You know I hate that nickname. The only time I could meet with the event coordinator is this morning and I'm already running behind."

"At least you're not stuck with a finance piece." He complains, his mouth setting in a firm line. "I can already feel myself dying inside. No one cares about another finance asshole telling people how to get rid of their debt."

I chuckle and mutter in agreement.

The revolving doors are in sight with my car parked on the curb visible through the glass. I was on my way out of town when I realized I left my voice recorder on my office desk. With a three-hour drive ahead of me and my meeting with the event coordinator happening in three hours, I'm pushing my luck.

"Yeah, have fun with that. See you in a week." I slap his shoulder before pushing through the doors of the building and starting my drive.

It's a quiet drive once I get out of the city and onto the two-lane interstate that will take me straight to Rose Prairie. Tall trees line either side of the winding road, a patchwork of yellows, reds, and oranges leaves as fall settles in. It almost makes me wish I had made different choices in my life.

After a peaceful drive, signs for Rose Prairie come into view. For a small town, it sure has a lot going for it. Gravel roads branch off the interstate with signs for pumpkin patches and hayrides. It's even got a small college, which seems to be waking up with young students looking sleepy-eyed as they trudge from their dorms as I pass by the campus.

The GPS guides me through the town square. A gazebo towers in the middle of the grassy square already in the process of getting decorated for the festival. Unlike the bustling city streets, people around here walk lazily on the sidewalk, stopping to chat with others on their way through town. Businesses with open signs blazing in the window fronts line the streets opposite the square making me think of those Hallmark movies my grandma would make me watch.

The address Miss Williams gave me after our brief conversation on the phone is a large metal green warehouse with a gravel driveway. A beat-up truck is already parked and

I pull in next to it. With only a short window of time to meet with Miss Williams, I'm lucky I was able to get here on time.

My first taste of fresh air in three hours is crisp and clean. Completely different from the stale gasoline-tinged air of the city. I take a moment to close my eyes, enjoying the sun on my face before gathering my supplies from the back seat.

A loud metallic bang startles me, my head nearly connecting with the roof of the car. I laugh at myself, shaking my head at being so jumpy as I shut the car door. A young woman with long dark hair wearing jeans and a flannel shirt is followed by a large man holding two hot drinks.

"You must be Miss Williams." I offer a hand to the woman as I introduce myself. "Matt Smith from *The Daily Click*. I go by Smith, so feel free to call me that. Thanks for meeting with me."

She smiles politely and takes my hand in a firm grasp. "Call me Sammie. This is Levi." She gestures to the man behind her. "He's my assistant."

"Carpenter." He corrects, nudging her shoulder playfully. "The one she's lucky to have." He hands the drinks out to Sammie and offers his hand. "She doesn't know what she'd do without me."

"I'd probably get more done," she mutters sarcastically under her breath with an eye roll. "Would you like a coffee? It's from our local shop in the town square."

Levi hands me the steaming cup and I take it offering my thanks. "Where should we start?"

Sammie and Levi guide me around the warehouse as they tell me how they both got involved with creating these events. Sammie was hired shortly before the Christmas Spectacular, the popular Christmas Eve event the town has thrown for generations. Levi was appointed to help her during the rush to get new decorations made, and the two of them pulled off the most successful Christmas Spectacular to date, which is how I ended up here.

"But now you're branching out?" I ask, gesturing to the work area we're standing in. The entire back half of the warehouse has rows of shelving, each one labeled with the corresponding event, the items carefully wrapped and stored in watertight containers.

"You could say that. My goal when I was hired by the board was to make Rose Prairie a place everyone wanted to visit. We did a Valentine's Day event that was a big hit, so I'm planning on adding more things; the Fall Festival being one of them."

"And you're finding the town supportive of that?"

Levi places an arm around Sammie's shoulders, pulling her close. "Absolutely. Sammie's done an amazing job at getting everyone in the town involved. She's the first person to reach out to Rosewood College, getting the art department to help with painting the decorations. She's amazing." Admiration shines through him as he looks down, their eyes locking before he kisses the top of her head. Witnessing the small act of affection transports me to another time, one that left its mark.

We end our interview with a walk through the town square. Sammie explains her process and how everything is going to be set up. Several volunteers wrap the light poles with fall garlands as we walk, our footsteps crunching on fallen leaves. I'll admit that she is passionate about these projects and I'm curious to see the turnout this Saturday.

"I appreciate your time. Thank you for meeting with me and showing me around. This will be great for the article." We stand under the shade of a large tree by the gazebo as I click off the recorder.

"You're welcome. I wish I had more time to give, but things are pretty busy these days. But I do have someone who volunteered to show you around Rose Prairie this week to help with your article, if that's okay."

"Oh, that'll be great," I say, giving her a polite smile. Since I'm here through Saturday, it'll be nice to have someone who can help me research my article.

"Perfect," she says, clapping her hands. "She's a business owner and has lived here most of her life, so she'll be great at helping. I can introduce you two before I head back."

There are still a couple of hours to go until I can check in to the bed-and-breakfast *The Daily Click* set me up with, so I agree. Might as well get more things done while I can.

Sammie leads me across the town square and toward the coffee shop called Tall, Dark, and Coffee. She smiles and waves at several people who offer friendly greetings and again I'm struck by how different this place is from the city.

Sammie holds out the door to the quaint shop, ushering me inside. A blast of that addicting coffee smell hits my face, the bell above the door dinging with our arrival. It's a cozy space with small tables sprinkled around the storefront with several college students busily typing away on their computers. Bookshelves ring the edges with genres posted that can be easily read from the main door. I chuckle to myself, noticing the much larger romance section that takes up the majority of the shelving space.

A young woman works at the counter busily making a drink for a waiting customer. The display case showcases an assortment of baked goods and some bottled drinks. A chalkboard hangs from the ceiling behind the barista listing their drink specialties and costs. It's a cute place that has a lot of charm with its aged red bricks and comfortable feel. I can see why it's the local favorite, the logo matches the one on the cup Levi offered me this morning and it was delicious.

Sammie walks up to the barista as I look around the place. I have a feeling I'm going to be spending some time here working on my article and chatting with the locals.

The barista says something about going to get someone before walking down the small hallway that no doubt leads to the private offices.

Sammie turns to me, a bright smile on her face. "Cara's great."

The name rings like a gong through my head, but I shake it off. Cara's not an uncommon name. Many people are named Cara. "Well, I appreciate her help." Curiosity wins out, and the question spills from my lips. "What's her last name, if you don't mind me asking?"

"Oh right, for your article. It's Moore. Cara Moore." As if on cue a familiar curvy silhouette appears down the hall walking confidently toward me.

My heart breaks out into a frantic rush, my mind picturing the beautiful face of my biggest regret as Cara walks down the hallway and freezes.

Chapter Three

Cara

It's him.

How can it be *him?*

My body jerks to a sudden stop, my eyes widening in disbelief. I never planned to see him again. Never thought he would come strolling back into my life. Not once did I dare to picture him standing in my coffee shop. Emotions I've long buried for him swirl under the surface of my skin, my arms breaking out in goosebumps at seeing Smith standing at the end of the hallway. Memories of the past wound me just as deeply now as they did all those years ago when I left.

I guess some wounds never heal.

Time slows as Smith and I stare at each other. To his credit, he looks just as shocked as I do, maybe more so. And damn him, he looks even better than the last time I saw him.

Smith has filled out, no longer the tall skinny twenty-two-year-old he was. He's still tall, but his figure is less lean and more defined. The white button-down and black jeans he's wearing fit him perfectly, accentuating his physic. But it's those blue eyes, the ones I see in my dreams, that haunt me the most as we stare at each other.

"There she is." Sammie cheers, her footsteps bouncy as she steps between us, snapping me out of my haze. "Cara, this is Smith, the journalist from *The Daily Click*." She gestures to the man I used to know who has the decency to look embarrassed.

"Smith, this is Cara, owner of Tall, Dark, and Coffee, who will show you around this week."

Smith swallows hard, his Adam's apple bobbing. "Cara." He tilts his head toward me. It's a good thing he didn't offer his hand because I don't know if I would've been able to take it.

Sammie glances between the two of us, her gaze questioning as she locks eyes with me. Cool disdain rolls off me in waves, my jaw set firm, willing no emotion into my features.

I've cried too much over this man already.

Six years isn't long enough.

"Okay, well..." Sammie trails off, her head bouncing like a tennis ball between us. "Cara, I'll call you later?" She gives me a pointed look and I nod, knowing she won't take no for an answer.

We stand awkwardly, feet apart, neither one of us saying a word. Customers shuffle in, the bell dinging in the background, the click of the register, and the low hum of customers filling the space between us.

Smith shuffles on his feet, his arm reaching between us like a peace offering. "Cara, I had no idea..." He runs his hand through the inky dark hair, a lone piece brushing against his forehead. "I'm happy to see you."

"Don't," I whisper, trying to keep my voice low so customers won't overhear. The last thing I need is for a rumor to spread through town. Deep calming breaths fill my chest as I try to regain my slipping composure. I don't think I can do this. I can't be this close to him. My mind flickers through who would be able to work with him while I hole myself in my office for several days until he leaves town.

Smith blinks his blue eyes at me, waiting for me to speak. He always had a way of knowing exactly how I was feeling at any given moment, and it seems that that's another thing time failed to lessen.

The list I was attempting to compile drifts from my mind like leaves in the fall breeze. I let out a slow exhale, steeling my spine for what I'm going to have to do. "This isn't going to be some walk down memory lane," I say firmly to both myself and to him. "No talking about the past or bringing up old baggage. I promised Sammie I'd show you around town, and believe me, if I hadn't already made all sorts of arrangements, I'd let you fend for yourself."

A whole helluva lot of me wants to shut the door behind him and never open it again. Go back to my life before he showed up in my town. Try to forget about him and all the feelings that resurface when I look at him. But it's time to push my own personal feelings to the side and focus on Rose Prairie.

"Cara," he sighs my name, flashbacks of that same sound from a different time flicker through my mind. Those ridiculous blue eyes beckon me closer, to close the gap between us like I long to do, but I hold my ground, willing my feet to stay planted. He holds up his hands in surrender before sliding them into his pockets. "Alright. Professional interactions only."

"Good." My arms cross under my chest, the embroidery of the logo on my apron digging into my forearms. "Meet me here tomorrow morning at nine," I instruct before turning on my heel and going back to my office.

HOT PLATES IS BUSY for a Monday night. The race car-themed restaurant offers made-to-order meals that taste homemade but better. Black and white tiled floors are accented by the bright red tables and chairs that are all full of customers. It's one of the few nice-ish places to eat in town—not that there are many options.

Looking around the restaurant, I see that June isn't here yet, which is normal. She works at Honey's Diner as a waitress and our dinners together help keep us sane in this town. She was the first friend I ever made in Rose Prairie and she's been by my side ever since.

It doesn't take long for the blonde beauty to walk in wearing her honey gold 60s-inspired uniform. I love her, but the girl is so unaware that she turns heads wherever she goes.

"So sorry I'm late. There was a table of college kids who wouldn't stop complaining about their cafeteria food," she huffs out in one breath as she plops in the seat across from me. "They tipped well though, so dinner's on me."

"Absolutely not," I snort. This is an ongoing argument we have every damn week. "It's my week to pay. You paid last week. I'm not going to let you." She tightens her ponytail and gives in with a giggle.

We place our orders, and I fill her in on my mess of a day. "You'll never guess who showed up in town today. Think blast from my past." The spinach and artichoke dip breaks my chip and I focus on digging out the fragment from underneath all the melted cheese.

Ice clinks in her glass as she hums to herself. "A blast from your past..." she trails off, her eyes going distant as she thinks. "Can you give me something else to go off of?"

Giving up on my search, I reach for another chip, biting into it with a satisfying crunch. "Ex," I mumble through a full mouth.

Her exclamatory gasp draws looks from around the restaurant. "Shut the front door! *Smith*?"

The familiar waitress, I think her name is Marianne, sets our plates in front of us, as she issues a warning about the hot plates. I thank her with a smile, recognizing her from my coffee shop. I think she bought a book yesterday now that I think about it. Would it be too weird to ask if she likes it? Maybe she's interested in joining our book club...

"The very one," I reply with a sigh as the waitress moves on to her next table. June was there for the fallout of my relationship with Smith all those years ago when I fled the city, my heart broken. An echo of pain ripples through my chest, the wound still fresh after all this time. I take a bite of my shrimp taco, the perfect combination of honey and spice mingling on my tongue. "And, you remember the journalist Sammie begged me to show around this week?" June's blue eyes widen as she nods her head, busy chewing on her steak. "Well, Smith *is* that journalist."

She takes her time mulling over the information, her brows furrowing as she chews. June sets her utensils down as she leans in beckoning me closer with a wave of her hand. "Should we cut his balls off?" she whispers deadpan, her serious question throwing me off. My composure breaks with a loud snort as I desperately suck in air as my body wracks with laughter. June stares at me for a beat, a bewildered expression on her face before she chuckles with me. "I was being serious," she explains when I finally manage to calm down. "I really think we should cut his balls off."

"I know you did. That's why it was so funny." June is my ride-or-die, and even though I've never told anyone what happened with Smith and me, she's willing to do anything if I ask.

"So wait, did you know it was going to be him when she asked you?"

I share my tumultuous story about seeing my ex-boyfriend walk into my coffee shop as we eat, occasionally stopping for June to ask questions. When I explain all the arrangements I made this week for *the journalist*, she stops me.

"Hold up. Let's think this through for a minute. Why don't you throw in some extra activities," she adds with air quotes. "You know, to get him off your back?"

My eyes narrow. "What are you thinking over there, June?"

She leans back against the bright red metal of her chair, sipping through her straw. "I don't know. Maybe throw in something unpleasant."

A very specific person comes to mind and excitement bubbles in my chest.

I know exactly what to do.

Chapter Four

Smith

The second I saw Cara, I knew I was going to try to win her back. How could I not when those honey-brown eyes flash in my mind every time I blink?

She looks amazing. I hadn't seen her in six years and still, the sight of her had my heart racing. Her generous curves, the way her jeans hugged her hips, and the way her lips parted in shock were almost more than my poor heart could handle. By the time I checked into the bed and breakfast after wandering around Cara's shop and speaking with locals, the overwhelming shock had dulled, but only by a fraction.

The Rosebranch Bed and Breakfast is a large white farmhouse wedged back in a picturesque prairie with tall grasses, which look like they're full of flowers during the spring. A large wrap-around porch features half a dozen rocking chairs and comfortable seating that looks out over the prairie. A shiny gold-plated sign by the door distinguishes the house as a historic Rose Prairie building.

The wide staircase creaks with every step down to the dining room, the enticing smell of bacon frying beckoning me closer. Several other guests are staying here this week and I'm greeted by the sound of knives scraping against plates as I reach the bottom step.

Hank and Darla Richards have owned and operated The Rosebranch Bed and Breakfast for the last forty years. They seem like a typical older couple who've been together forever. Hank is quiet and stoic while Darla is warm and welcoming. The minute I stepped through the door she wrapped in a hug only a grandmother could give. She made sure I knew when breakfast was and that she was known around town for her cooking skills, and based on the aromas seeping through the swinging doors from the kitchen, I bet she wasn't lying.

The long dining table is set up for breakfast. Pitchers of juice and coffee sit in the middle of the table ready for guests to pour. A middle-aged couple sits side by side talking quietly while they sip their coffee. Places are set with white china with orange and yellow decorative napkins resting across the plates bundled by silver napkin rings. Several other guests are seated, spread out along the banquet table quietly eating their breakfast and reading the local newspaper.

"Good morning," I greet everyone with a soft smile, that stubborn piece of hair bouncing over my forehead. A chorus of polite responses greets me as I take my seat.

Footsteps creak on the old hardwood floor as the swinging door opens. Darla walks into the dining room with a smile, her hands loaded with plates of steaming food. "Well good morning, young man." Darla places a fresh plate of delicious-looking breakfast food in front of the older man sitting next to me. "We've got a very important journalist staying with us," she tells the table. "Did you sleep well dear?" Her delicate hand pats my shoulder.

"I did." The white lie is smooth as honey as it slips from my lips. I didn't sleep a wink last night. The sight of Cara standing in front of me, talking to me, was playing on repeat in my mind.

Darla quickly runs through the breakfast menu, occasionally stopping to give me her advice before I place my order. With a flick of her pen and a gentle pat on the shoulder, she leaves the table, the door to the kitchen swinging behind her.

"Journalist, huh?" The older gentleman next to me turns in my direction as Darla skitters into the kitchen. I pour myself a steaming mug of coffee that I hope will settle my nerves, and nod at the man. He's got a tanned face that reminds me of someone who's spent most of their life working in the sun. Lines cut valleys along his cheeks, emphasized by the impressive handlebar mustache resting under his large nose. "From the looks of ya, you come from the city. What's a city slicker doin' in our neck of the woods?"

I smile politely at the older gentleman. "What's wrong with my look?" I thought my dark jeans and green henley were appropriate casual attire. Not to mention, I remember how much Cara loved my henleys.

His dark eyes crinkle as he chuckles. "Nothin'. Just says city is all."

"Huh," I huff, my eyes squinting at his observation. "I'm Smith." I offer him my hand and he takes it in his strong grip. Large calluses scrape against my hand, noting his decades of hard work. He introduces himself as Culver. "I'm here to do a story about Rose Prairie. Specifically, I'm learning about the town and the events that have started to gain notoriety. If you don't mind me asking, what brings you to Rose Prairie? I'd like to learn why people enjoy visiting."

The woman across from us catches my eye as she takes a sip of her orange juice. She's leaning forward in her seat, her hand casually pulling her hair behind her ear before tilting her head in our direction.

Culver sucks his teeth. "That's a complicated question. The standard answer is that I used to work here some thirty years ago and thought a visit would be nice."

"And the real reason?" I prod gently. Part of being a journalist is learning how to read people. Culver seems like a nice man, but there's a shadow to him like he's troubled by something.

"Off the record, hotshot." I hold out my hands in surrender and he chuckles. "Old flame. Heard she's a widower now. Like you, I heard about this town, and like a light going off I had this feeling." His hand rests against his heart, tapping lightly. "A pull telling me I needed to come back."

"Oh my gosh, that's beautiful." The woman across from us puts a hand against her throat before she clears it. "I'm sorry for interrupting, but I couldn't help but overhear." She rests her hand against her husband's forearm, her ring glinting in the morning light. "I'm Cheryl, this is my husband Hugh." The husband in question dips his chin in acknowledgment. "Would you be interested in our story?" Her face beams as I smile politely, inclining my head for her to continue. "We were married at The Lookout fifteen years ago. We planned to come earlier when the meadow would be full of beautiful prairie roses, but life had other plans." Her blue eyes mist over and Hugh places a reassuring arm across her shoulders. "Anyway, we had to put off our trip until now. But I love seeing all of the beautiful fall trees and I'm happy that we're going to get to stay for the festival."

Darla walks in with a steaming plate and sets it in front of me. Blueberry pancakes are stacked high resting beside homemade hash browns, bacon, and eggs making my mouth water. "Did I hear you talking about the festival? I think it's just great that Ms. Williams has come in and transformed our little town. She's got everyone involved. I think she's really creating something special here."

More guests make their way down for breakfast joining our conversation and giving me plenty of information to use in my article. One younger couple was passing through and decided to stop and visit the pumpkin patch I saw a sign for on my way in. They enjoyed their time so much, they decided to extend their stay.

In the back of my mind, I know that this wouldn't be happening if I were staying in a hotel in the city. People mind their own business, oftentimes overlooking everyone else. Does this kind of thing happen everywhere, or is this special to Rose Prairie?

Plate scraped clean, I glance at my watch. Time flies when you're having a good conversation. The soft laughter of the group follows behind me as I step out the front door and onto the wooden porch.

Time to go try to win Cara back.

CARA WORKS BEHIND THE counter, smiling as she greets her customers. I'm standing in the back of the line, hidden from view by the patrons in front of me, so I take the opportunity to look at her. Truly look at her for the first time in over five years.

She moves with confidence and grace behind the counter; her smile never leaving her face. Did she smile like that all those years ago? I can't remember. Cara seems to glow, entirely in her element, naturally pulling people toward her. Her brown hair, longer than it had been, swings down between her shoulder blades in a ponytail, cascading down her neck. Her ears are studded with multiple piercings, including a bar going from one side of her ear to the other. The green apron settled across her front does nothing to hide the curves underneath, but it's her face that captures my attention.

I suck in a ragged breath, replacing the air knocked from my lungs at her beauty. Her naturally tan skin exudes youth, her cheeks a healthy pink. Those honey eyes, the same eyes I can't forget, are rimmed with dark lashes, and they glimmer with joy as she laughs with a younger woman.

Was I that much of an idiot that I let this woman slip through my fingers? Could I not see what was right in front of me?

The fact is that I did see what I had. I just don't know how I lost it.

Cara still hasn't noticed me as the line shortens. She's so beautiful and carefree, completely in her element. A soft smile pulls at my lips as I watch her work, emotions welling up in my chest. The sight of her, and the memory of how she left me, has me pulling my gaze away and toward the people lingering in the shop.

Customers chat quietly as they gaze out the front windows, looking out toward the town square. Parents walk hand-in-hand with children through the autumn leaves, backpacks happily bouncing on their backs. Looking around, I can see why this small town is talked about. It has this incredible sense of community, the kind where everyone knows everyone, where people help out without asking questions. The kind that some people search their whole lives for.

"Are you in line?" A woman's voice asks from behind my shoulder and I spin on my heel to look at her. I hadn't really gotten in line. I wanted to look at Cara with her walls down, without a stoic mask settled onto her delicate features.

I motion her forward, an apologetic smile on my face. "Go ahead." She thanks me quietly as she steps into the gaping space between me and the line.

Cara is still bustling behind the counter, her laughter drifting over to me and I'm hit with the realization that I once thought I'd never hear that sound again. A subtle warmth settles in my chest and I find myself chuckling quietly to myself shaking my head as I walk over to bookshelves, mindlessly picking up the first book my fingers touch.

Images of Cara laying in my bed, hair unbound and resting at her shoulders, the tiny strap to her silken top hanging off her shoulder as she reads her latest romance novel flood my mind. She always loved reading and I'd often walk into my bedroom, having spent most of the evening at work to find her there. Cozy as a bug in a rug, I'd say.

More images come to mind, cherished memories of our time together. The way her mouth would fall open when I kissed my way down her body. The playful glint in her eye when she issued another childish challenge that neither of us could refuse. The way her hair shone in the sunlight as we sat outside at a coffee shop, its rays creating a halo around her.

"Find something you like? You know, I always thought you would read my books when I wasn't there." The book in my hand shifts into focus, the half-naked man with completely unrealistic muscles flexing through his ripped shirt. I clear my throat nervously, shifting on my feet as I place the book back on the shelf.

She's leaning on her elbow against the bookcase, a satisfied smirk on her face at catching me off guard. Gone is the green apron and I can't stop my eyes from traveling down her gorgeous body.

"Never did have the time," I sigh. "But I remember what came *after* the reading." She swallows hard and I chuckle to myself, knowing full well what we are both picturing right now. "That one looks interesting." I point to the overly dramatic cover of the book I just put down to change the subject. The Cara in front of me today isn't the same one as yesterday. She's calmer, the hint of what used to be glimmering in her eyes. "I might have to buy it to see what all this romance stuff is about."

She straightens, crossing her arms across her chest. "Then you'll be happy to hear it's our latest book club pick. It's a shame you can't join." Her eyes narrow and her jaw juts stubbornly.

"Something to think about," I say, tapping the cover with a dull thump.

She rolls her shoulders slightly and glances out the window to the town square beyond it. It's the only outward sign of her discomfort and it has me stifling my grin. It was one of her tells that told me something brewed underneath her beautiful skin. I could always figure out how she felt about something based on that tiny little movement and she always got mad at me, especially when she had no idea she did it.

"Well, are you ready?"

I grab the strap of my bag and tug at it. "Just waiting on you."

God, if she only knew how true those words are.

Chapter Five

Cara

Smith's shoulder brushes against mine as we walk down the sidewalk. I purposefully quicken my steps, but Smith snorts a laugh and lengthens his stride. Our breaths create puffs of fog and I pull my jacket tighter around me to keep back the chill. It's the time of year that has our mornings cold enough to make you want to stay huddled in bed but warm enough in the afternoons that it's too gorgeous to stay indoors.

We're bathed in the warm sun, the scent of fall lingering in the breeze, and I wish I could bask in it, but I can't. Not when Smith keeps glancing my way. He's trying to play it off like he's admiring the buildings, but I can tell.

"Are you going to tell me where you're taking me, or is that for you to know and me to find out?" The corners of his mouth tilt up playfully as he looks down at me, blue eyes shining. It's the kind of look I used to love getting from him. The kind that says so much without a word being uttered. Soft and loving, but with a hint of challenge.

Damn him for bringing up our past this morning. Now all I can think about are the memories I've buried deep. Kept buried to stop from feeling my heart being ripped from my chest.

Before I left, Smith was the man of my dreams. The man that I spent my whole life longing for and always believed was too good to be true. Smith brought me to life. We brought each other to life, always playing and laughing with one another. It could have something to do with being young and in love, but already I'm starting to feel that comfortable familiarity wrapping around us. Having him so close has me letting my guard down.

My steps falter, so caught up in this gaze, and I blink rapidly to shake off these feelings coming back to the surface. "You could say that," my voice is low and deadpan as I place my cold hands in the pockets of my jacket.

It actually is like that. My carefully laid plan that June helped me concoct at our dinner last night is about to be put into action.

We've come to a stop at the intersection of Main Street and wait for the little blinking man to appear before we cross. Smith reaches across me to push the button, his cologne lingering in the cold air, and I have to fight to keep my eyes open. To not make a fool of myself for breathing in and losing myself in it.

He chuckles softly, shaking his head. "Why do I feel like this is a trap?" He swivels his head toward me, blue eyes squinted against the sun.

"I have no idea what you're talking about," I reply innocently.

"Right," he murmurs. "You forget I know you."

The loud beeping from the crosswalk startles me, making me jump. Smith's large hand settles on the small of my back and I can't breathe as he leads me to the other side, not dropping his hand until I'm safely on the sidewalk.

First, he's bringing up old memories, and now this? He's knocking me off balance this morning, and I'm not sure I can handle it. I've kept Smith in a sealed box, locked away with no intention of opening it back up again, but now that he's here, that lid has been blown wide open.

Maybe June was right and we should just cut off his balls and be done with it.

Lucky for me, it's a quick walk to our final destination and Smith stays blissfully quiet. The community center is an old brick building across the street from the town hall and is already bustling with people. Rose Prairie Community Center offers all sorts of extra-curricular activities for students to join, and gives the retired community a place to hang out, which is precisely why we're here.

Smith raises an eyebrow at me as he scans the rows of tables. He leans in close, his breath whispering across my skin. "Is this where you kill me? I hate to break it to you, but there are far too many witnesses."

Without thinking, my hand smacks against the firmness of his stomach in a move that was once second nature. "No," I chuckle, trying and failing to not think about what he's packing under that damn henley. The green ribbed fabric showcases the broadness of his chest and shoulders, hugging his clearly defined physique. Did he wear this on purpose?

I have to admit that my mind was on Smith as I got dressed this morning, remembering how he loved scanning down my body when I wore fitted jeans. But jeans and a Tall, Dark, and Coffee t-shirt are my normal work attire, and his eyes still managed to flick over my body. Repeatedly. I clear my throat as I try to get my mind off that damn shirt and roll my shoulders.

"There's someone here who I know is *dying* to meet you," I tell him as I scan the crowd. She doesn't even know about him, but she would be tearing this town apart looking for him if she did, so my exaggeration isn't too far off.

Like clockwork, Lori Haverford, the town's most enthusiastic and downright nosy resident, spots a new face in town and I can see the moment she locks in on Smith. My cheeks ache from holding back a maniacal grin. "Oh, there she is." I point across the room to the older woman, now parting the crowd like the Red Sea.

Lori Haverford is a born and bred Rosie and she's proud of this town and the people in it. She might have an odd way of showing it, always in everyone else's business, but the woman does care for the people here. In her own way, that is. There were many times this past winter that Sammie would vent to me about "that busybody" when Lori would inevitably show up unannounced to give her critique on her hard work.

"Cara." Lori reaches out her hand to me before wrapping me in a hug. She must be in a good mood today because this is a rare greeting. Usually, it's more of a quick, curt nod. "And who is this handsome young man?" Her whole focus is entirely on Smith.

Exactly like we planned.

"Smith," he answers, offering his hand to her. "I'm a journalist from *The Daily Press,* here to write an article about Rose Prairie."

And there it is. I may appear calm, cool, and collected, but inside I'm doing cartwheels.

Lori loves nothing more than talking about this town and Smith just offered her the biggest platform.

"You don't say," she gasps. "Isn't this just wonderful?" She looks at me and I nod enthusiastically, knowing exactly where this will go. "Well, you've come to the right place, young man. How long are you here?" Her head tilts expectantly at Smith.

His blue eyes glance over at me. "Well, Cara was just telling me that you were wanting to meet me. I'm not sure how long we have."

The smile I've been holding back slides across my face in a shit-eating grin. "He's all yours." She doesn't hesitate to grab him by the arm and pull him through the crowd.

"So Smith," I hear her say as she pulls him away. Smith cranes his neck over his shoulder to look at me, a dark strand of hair bouncing over his forehead, his eyes squinting suspiciously as I laugh.

There's absolutely no chance that Smith is going to slip through her grasp anytime soon. If I know anything about Lori, it's that she would do anything for this town, and dragging a journalist whose job it is to listen while she rambles on emphatically about it? Shit, I kind of wish I was there to witness that brand of torture.

With a wicked grin, I snap a picture of Smith to send to June. My ex nods his head politely as he listens to Lori, but his gaze flickers over to me.

Those eyes? Burning. The blue flames blazing in them work to revive that nearly dying ember buried in my chest.

SOMETHING IS CALMING about being in the coffee shop after it's closed for the night. The stillness is peaceful. Most of my best thinking happens after the last customer leaves and there's nothing and no one to distract me. Warm lights drift over the book section, the fairy lights twinkling, and the combination of the darkness coupled with the glow works to settle me.

But not enough it seems.

It's the second time my newly formed book club is meeting and for some reason, I find myself more nervous now than I was last week. It was simple enough to rope June, Scarlet, and Mariah into joining. They're my friends and it's nice that they didn't put up too much of a fight when I begged them to join. Especially when I told them we would be reading *dirty* books. But it's everyone else who's making me bounce anxiously in my seat. The paperback novel we're reading flops against my knee with a dull thud as I try to get rid of the anxious energy.

The women gather around the snack table, chatting animatedly while they get their coffee and tea. Everyone brings something to contribute and from the looks of it, the cookies Scarlet brought are a hit.

What if they don't like it?

Wendy, Elle, and Tiffany are my wildcards. We've known each other since we were in our middle school days, but they seemed a tad reserved when we picked our book. I know that Rose Prairie isn't a big smut-loving crowd, but I'm hoping I can win them over.

As far as I know, there's never been a romance book club in this tiny town. Not that I'm going to ask. The only person who would have any clue is Lori Haverford and there's *no way* I'm opening that can of worms.

The thought of Lori has me grinning like a villain. I'm positive Lori didn't let Smith out of her sight, or earshot, until she told him the town's history, most likely paired with a lovely guided tour.

June catches my eye and gives a quirk of her brow, her lips pulling up in the corners with shared laughter. She knows exactly what's going through my head right now. She's the one who helped me plan it.

"It's weird being back," Scarlet says as I focus back on the group's conversation. "But Mom said she needed help, so here I am." She blows a wayward strand of hair back from her face. She's in the process of moving back and from the looks of her, she's been busy today. Her brown hair is in messy space buns with loose strands dangling over her face.

Scarlet and her mother Barbara own Mama's Cakes Bakery. They inherited it from her grandmother when she passed away. Scarlet, like most of us, needed time away from Rose Prairie, and her coming back to town has the rumor mill buzzing.

"If you need help, you know Barry can always come by." Tiffany offers as she attempts to cool off her steaming mug of tea.

Scarlet gives her a polite smile. "Thanks, but I've got it. No point in getting help now that the truck's unloaded."

We chat for a bit longer before we finally settle on book talk. This right here is what I was nervous about. The particular book we picked out comes highly recommended by multiple book sites, and like Smith pointed out, the man on the cover is... enticing. We all agreed on this choice, but I'm unsure what the others will think. This book starts with a bang. Quite literally.

"This book is hot," Wendy adds casually as she fans herself. "You might have ruined me for other books, Cara. Because damn."

"It's definitely sexy, but does anyone else think it's a bit creepy? They just met and already he's like *you're mine.*" Mariah dips her chin, lowering her voice in a terrible rendition of a man's deep rumble.

"You're supposed to suspend reality," I laugh. "Real world? Hell yeah, it's creepy as shit. Book world? He could say the most heinous things and I'd roll over." I slip down my chair, my arms going limp around me showing just how I'd melt. A chorus of agreement rings out, drowning out the jingle of the bell on the front door. "There's a reason why we call them book boyfriends. They're so much better than real life."

"I don't know," a distinctly male voice interjects, startling us all. My head whips over, my eyes locking with Smith as he leans casually on a bookshelf, the very same book we're reading dangling from his long fingers. "There are some things a book boyfriend can't do if I recall." His eyes narrow, taunting me.

"I'm sure there's a great many things you don't recall," I grind out through clenched teeth, not nearly loud enough for the group to hear.

Elle stands, flipping her light red hair over her shoulder before offering Smith her hand. "Hi," her voice seems to shoot up an entire octave as she introduces herself to my ex and I repress the urge to roll my eyes. "I'm Elle. Are you in our book club too?"

Jesus.

"No," I say at the same time Smith says yes. I stand, ready to push him out the door if I need to.

He's laying on all the charm, sucking them all into his orbit. "Yes," he repeats with a hard look at me before glancing back at Elle. "I am. Cara mentioned you were reading this book this morning and I couldn't help myself." He holds the book up for everyone to see. "Did I miss anything?"

"Like you actually read it," I scoff, flopping back down into my chair and crossing my arms mumbling to myself. "The Smith I knew never had time for stuff like that." Curious eyes glance at me, but I ignore them.

"After my wonderful day with Mrs. Haverford, I managed to come back here and buy that copy I was looking at earlier. I read the first five chapters." He runs his thumb across the paper edge, the pages flipping. "I can see why you were always reading."

If he's looking for some sort of reaction out of me, he's going to be sorely disappointed. Stone cold, baby.

Elle assures him that we've just started and that he didn't miss anything important. She does more than assure him. She hangs all over him and I try to push back the sting of jealousy. The other ladies introduce themselves and Scarlet pulls over a chair as I watch this train wreck about to happen.

How did he know? He said that I told him we were reading this book, but I didn't tell him when my book club was, right? I watch as he settles into his seat, my eyes wandering over the expanse of his chest in that damn shirt again.

June nudges me with her shoulder. "Are you okay," she whispers in my ear. Her eyebrows are raised in concern.

Smith watches me with a triumphant grin on his stupid, handsome face while Elle drums up conversation. "Oh yeah," I say full of sarcasm. "I'm peachy."

After the novelty of Smith arriving wears off, I do my best to completely ignore his presence. This is *my* book club. I'm not going to let him win this one. Maybe I deserve it after my stunt with Lori, and now this is my punishment. On second thought, no. That was well-deserved and honestly helpful. He would've had to talk with Lori eventually. I just helped him get it out of the way sooner.

Look at me being all helpful.

We settle back into talking about the book, this time with more focus on the plot and less time spent discussing our sexy new book boyfriend. The more we discuss, the more I realize that Smith *did* actually read it.

"I'm not so sure," Smith interjects. We're on the topic of the main character, Viv, who pushes the sexy bad boy Lark away after an emotionally stressful scene. "I agree that some space was needed, but to leave him high and dry without an explanation. Or a simple conversation," he shakes his head.

I lean forward in my seat. "So you're suggesting what?" I argue. "She was too emotionally distraught to have a conversation like that with him, so she did what she thought was best. She left. He's a big boy, he can handle it."

Scarlet and Tiffany back me up, each offering their point of view.

"Running's going to get her nowhere." Smith leans forward in his chair, mirroring my stance.

"I'm pretty sure it gets her away from him," I snort sarcastically. One of the best things to do in situations like that, when emotions are overwhelming, is to find some sort of escape. I should know. "Sometimes people need a breather. Her leaving gave her that." Viv is a character I can appreciate and relate to. She knows what's best for her at that moment and does it, damn the consequences.

Smith rubs his hand along his jaw. "She could have been an adult about it and had an adult conversation before disappearing. It could've saved them both from the heartache that's clearly coming." His eyes lock with mine, and I know we're not talking about Viv. His words sting, slicing into my already wounded heart.

Because we're not talking about Viv or Lark.

We're talking about us.

"Maybe her running was her way of avoiding that heartbreak." The women sitting in the circle around are wide-eyed as Smith and I dig through our past trauma under the guise of talking about a book.

"No," he states firmly. "Her leaving was the worst possible thing she could do."

My head shakes, a wan smile settling across my features. "You don't get it."

Smith stands abruptly, his voice pleading. "Then explain it to me." That dark strand of hair bounces on his forehead and he runs a hair through his midnight tresses. He looks as if all his energy was sucked away with that one movement, and he sighs. "Explain why you left."

The entire room is eerily silent as Smith and I stare at each other. The heater kicks on, the dull whirring the only noise in the room. They'd have to be blind to not see that Smith and I were no longer talking about fictional characters, arguing about a fictional plot point. We were both stuck in our hurt, reliving and arguing parts of our past.

Tears sting my eyes and I blink rapidly at the floor to keep them at bay, breaking the tense connection with Smith. June's hand glides up and down my back as I try to regain my composure.

Unable to look back at him, I hear the soft rustling of fabric and the scrape of a chair. He clears his throat to break the awkward silence. "I apologize for ruining such a nice night. Ladies, please forgive me. Cara," his voice breaks on my name, "I'm sorry."

When I manage to glance up, he's already gone.

Chapter Six

Smith

I'm tucked into the largest booth at Honey's Diner, surrounded by local business owners. Cara was the last one to arrive, and after last night, I don't blame her.

When I finally managed to pry myself away from Mrs. Haverford after an eventful—and long—conversation full of tangents, I spotted the sign in the window for Cara's book club and I knew what I had to do. Hadn't she told me that morning the exact book they were reading? After the stunt she pulled on me, I thought I needed to issue my own form of payback. Just like old times.

But I was out of line. And it might have ruined whatever hope I have of winning her back.

Last night, everything came flooding back. Cara left me without a word. Completely cut me off and out of her life without a hint of explanation. Just...gone. A black hole had taken over my life, become my heart and soul, and last night, the veil covering that hole had ripped free, leaving me raw and bleeding. It was too much.

Having Cara sitting there, finally giving an inkling as to why she left and taking my heart with her, dragged everything buried deep back to the surface.

I fucked up.

She looked so sad, her golden eyes filled with tears. It's the first outward sign of any emotions toward me. But I can't figure out the reason behind them. Everything that happened six years ago continues to be a mystery to me.

What happened last night is making the atmosphere between us more tense than it has been, and I need to fix it. I need that snarky, playful Cara back. *We* need that back, especially if I'm going to win her back. And I will win her back. There's no other option for me. I need to remind her of what we used to be—and could still be.

She's refusing to look at me, to turn those gorgeous eyes in my direction and settle this feeling in my chest. Cara loosens her shoulders before rolling her neck and letting out an audible sigh. Her long hair catches my eye as it slips behind her neck, dancing over skin I know to be smooth as silk, utterly distracting me. It's a good thing my recorder rests in the middle of the table because my eyes, and attention, are glued to Cara.

"—booming. It's a shame when things slow back down after a rush like that." Cooper, the owner of Eatin' Good shakes his head, his hands sitting heavy on the table. Plates clinking, ice sloshing, and the low murmur of the restaurant linger around us as all eyes turn to me.

Shit, what had I asked?

Managing to drag my eyes away from Cara without her noticing, I clear my throat as I brush that damn lock of hair off my forehead. "So the publicity helps, but only for a moment?" I ask, and heads nod around the table.

"It's also brought in new businesses into town as well," Scarlet, co-owner of the bakery who I recognize from last night's fiasco, adds. "Right now they're building another chain down the road, I saw it on my drive back into town the other day."

"Oh, that's right," Margi agrees, her short white hair bobbing as she nods. "I had heard that they were building something off Hodge Street, but I didn't know what it could be. Surely this town only needs one kitchenware store, right?" Her kind, wrinkled face is etched in concern as she scans the table. Cara reaches over and gently rubs her shoulder, giving her comfort.

"We will all be fine," Cara adds, the jut of her chin and the fierce look in her eyes conveying her confidence as she locks eyes with her peers. "No one is going to shut down or close businesses. Rose Prairie won't let that happen."

"So would you say this town looks out for each other?" My question hangs in the air, not directed at any one person, but my gaze is locked on Cara, begging her to look at me. Hell, even the raise of her middle finger in my direction would be a welcome sight at this point.

"Of course we do." Cara slowly turns toward me, her voice softening from the fierce tone from earlier. "That's what makes Rose Prairie different from any other place. The people have so much heart and loyalty."

Those honey eyes fill with pride as she speaks about her town and as they flicker over my face, I feel myself relax into them. That sense of panic at her cutting me off melts until it's nothing but a memory.

"I agree," Scarlet nods. "I spent years away from this place and the moment I come back, the people never fail to leave me in awe. Why do you think we all come back?" She nudges Cara with a playful grin. "In the city, people stick to themselves and stay within their bubble, not thinking about where they get their bagel every morning. Our community does, plain and simple."

"You speak for the established businesses though," I counter, wanting to make sure everyone has a say. "What about newer businesses that come in without the backing of the community? What then?" My eyes bounce from person to person, some of them sitting stoically as they contemplate my question.

A throat clears in the corner of the booth. "It's hard." Cooper leans forward, his elbows on the table, his eyes downcast. "Don't get me wrong, opening a new business is difficult everywhere, but getting a foot up here?" His head shakes to emphasize his point. "It was hard as hell. My deli opened in January and I still see locals walk by without a second glance. I've got to thank those college kids though, 'cause they almost single-handedly keep me open."

Our meeting lasted for several hours, going from a relaxed interview to discussions on how to work better together as a community. Sammie stopped in during lunch and her brow scrunched in thought as she took in what everyone had to say. Many thanked her for getting them involved in her projects, which she brushed off with a wave before heading back to work on the Fall Festival set up.

The firm set to Cara's shoulders loosens the longer the meeting lasts and I'm glad for it. I need to get us back on solid ground after the rift that halted any progress I had deluded myself into thinking I made.

Several owners mingle after the meeting ends, and I grab my stuff and start packing up. I can't stop myself from watching Cara as she hugs Scarlet with a tight squeeze before turning to the door. My movements pick up, carelessly tossing my notebook and recorder into my bag and scrambling out of the booth.

Is she running? Cara moves like a gazelle and is already halfway to her car by the time my foot hits the pavement. "Cara," I call after her, hoping she'll slow her pace. My bag bounces on my shoulder as I jog to catch up to her right as she slams her car door shut. "Cara." I try again, my knuckles bouncing off the solid window a little too hard. "Shit," I curse, waving my throbbing hand in the air to dull the pain. "I was hoping to talk to you." She snorts at my pain but rolls down her window.

"Don't go hurting yourself, Smith. I wouldn't want you injuring your writing hand."

To show her how uninjured I am, I raise my middle finger towards her. "I think I'll be fine." She huffs out a laugh, her smile tugging at the corners, and for once, I wish she'd direct that smile at me.

"Did you come over here to flip me off or..." she gestures for me to continue. Right, this probably isn't the best way to get her to loosen up.

"I've heard about the pumpkin patch down the road and thought I should check it out. Someone mentioned pumpkin carving and thought maybe you'd like to join me. You know, make a friendly competition out of it. If you have the time, that is." *Please say yes*, I beg. If I could get some one-on-one time, and get her to let her guard down, then maybe I stand a chance.

Cara clicks her tongue, her eyes squinting up at me as she weighs my offer. The Cara I knew would never back down from a challenge, especially one that involved me. "Alright, Smith.

Let's see what you're made of." She flicks her chin to the right. "Get in."

I waste no time and hop in the passenger seat before she can change her mind and speed away. Cara leans over and turns the radio up before I can utter a single word.

So much for getting her to talk to me.

The drive out of town into the farmlands doesn't take long, but I use the time to study the woman next to me. How is she this stunning?

Wearing a magenta sweater and leggings, she looks like heaven. Even more, she looks like home. The sweater clings to her hips and chest like a glove showcasing her neck-breaking curves. Suddenly, my mouth is dry and my palm tingles as I fight the urge to reach over and caress her thigh. It had once been a reflex to reach across the expanse of the center console and run my fingers along her inner thigh as she drives. Although it's been six years without her, the longing is still there.

Perhaps she can sense the change in my thoughts because she glances my way, her eyebrow raised. The sun streaming through the windshield washes her in a golden ray, its beams like a beacon pointing directly at what—who—I want most. "Stop being a creeper," she shouts over the stereo.

"I'm not creeping," I argue, turning back to look at the sprawling country road. I was creeping, but that doesn't mean I need to let her know that. "I thought I saw a deer on that side." I'm not completely lying. I had seen a deer, but that was when I first drove into town.

"You're such a liar," she laughs, shaking her head.

We reach the turn-off I passed on my drive-in, the sign for the pumpkin patch pointing down the gravel drive. The rumble of tires on gravel drowns out all but the dinging hits of the rocks on the undercarriage. Cars leaving our destination pass us slowly and before long, rows and rows of pumpkins lie in fields on both sides of the road, families carefully searching for their perfect pumpkin.

Cara pulls into the dirt parking lot and wastes no time getting out of the car. I shake my head, smiling to myself as I step out of her car.

If it didn't feel like fall before, it certainly does now. Somehow the air out here is more crisp and we're only several miles outside of town. I can't help but breathe deeply, letting the scent of fall settle my nerves. Cara waits for me outside the entry gates and I watch as she rolls her shoulders as I approach. Her eyes follow me until I come to a stop beside her.

Now who's being a creeper?

"You ready to get your ass whooped?" Reaching into my wallet, I pay the attendant at the booth.

Cara walks past me, turning sharply on her heel, her arms spread out wide as she walks backward. "I think you've got that all wrong, mister. If I recall correctly, your knife skills are severely lacking."

"Oh really? How much you wanna bet?"

She stops, narrowing her eyes. The space between us seems to electrify as she eyes me up and down, her gaze scrutinizing the challenge in my eyes. "Alright," she clicks her tongue, "the loser has to wear their pumpkin on their head all *Sleepy Hollow*-like."

"Deal." My hand stretches out between us. "But the loser has to walk around the pumpkin patch, it can't be a quick on-off thing. Plus," I add, "he never actually wore the jack-o'-lantern as his head."

She shrugs her shoulders before her delicate hand slides into mine. "Semantics. It's not going to really matter when you lose."

Chapter Seven

Cara

I don't think Smith knows what he's getting himself into. Doesn't he remember that I grew up in this town, coming to this very same pumpkin patch year after year, and have carved many a pumpkin in my time?

This is going to be fantastic.

"Someone's a little cocky today," he murmurs as we hunt through the rows of pumpkins to find the perfect one. It has to be large enough to fit over our heads, or rather, *his* head.

I bend down, grabbing the stem of the gigantic pumpkin, spinning it to see if it's the perfect one. "Not cocky," I amend, as I wrap my arms around the oversized orange gourd and attempt to lift it. "Confident."

The smooth surface of the pumpkin does nothing to help me lift it, the fabric of my sweater gliding over it like it's been greased before landing with a thump. "At least I didn't get it off the ground, otherwise I would've ruined a perfectly good pumpkin," I mumble to myself as I try again to wrap it in my arms and lift. Did someone come out here and slather this thing in Crisco? I push myself out of my crouch and stand, examining the stubborn ass gourd. "Oh no, you are not going to beat me," I let the pumpkin know as I roll up my sleeves before crouching once more. With one final tug, the pumpkin lifts from the ground and into my arms. "Ha, victory."

"Are you done here? As happy as I am to see that you're able to defeat a pumpkin, I'm ready for a little competition." Smith stands to my left, a large pumpkin cradled in the crook of his elbow.

Why does he look like he's shooting a damn magazine cover? Blue jeans and a black shirt covered by a yellow flannel with the sleeves rolled up his strong forearms, muscles flexing as he adjusts the pumpkin in his grip. I've been fighting the constant attraction I have for him, but he keeps doing things to make me break my focus. Looking at him is like watching a car crash—I know I shouldn't look because it will only bring pain, but I can't look away.

Through sheer force of will, I drag my eyes away from him, only lingering on his chest and arms for a moment. Again, why does he have to look so damn good?

"Now who's arrogant?" I point out, readjusting the pumpkin in my arms. The damn thing is heavier than it looks and I'm worried it'll slip right out of my grasp and land with a splat if I don't set it down soon. I walk past him, heading toward the pumpkin carving stands. "Time to eat your words, big guy."

The nickname I used for him leaves my mouth as smooth as velvet and without a thought. I whisper a silent prayer that Smith didn't catch my slip-up or the face I made when I caught myself. It's just so easy to fall back into what used to be. He's bringing up all the good feelings and memories of our time together, and it's starting to mess with my head.

Families of all ages are running around the pumpkin patch, little ones barely able to walk carry baby pumpkins around in their fat little fists refusing to let anyone hold them. Older children laugh as they climb on the hay bale fort and young couples take pictures on the oversized rocking chair. Shouts come from the corn maze, their laughter-tinged voices drifting through the wind.

Smith follows close behind me under the awning and into the pumpkin carving pavilion. The pumpkin in my arms lands with a clunk on the table at the entrance in front of the volunteer working the carving station, who greets us cheerfully, all smiles and perky voice. Smith sets his down gently with a smirk at me before reaching into his wallet.

Quick as lightning, I grab his wrist resting on the pumpkin, halting his movements. "Let me pay for the pumpkins. You paid for us to get in. Plus, it's the least I could do before I win." Those blue eyes like shining sapphire meet mine and for a moment, there's no one else around. Gone are the families, the laughing children. It's just me and him, his skin under my palm.

His eyes search my face before he nods with barely a tilt of his chin. I swallow hard, letting his wrist slide free of my grasp as I pay for our oversized pumpkins.

The young attendant wearing a purple beanie takes my money before gesturing to the rows of tables. "You can choose your station. At each one is a book of references that you can look at, or you can create your own style, which is always fun. Everything you'll need is there, as well as trash cans for the guts." Her face scrunches in disgust before morphing back into a cheerful smile. "We will use the seeds for next year's crop so people can come back every year to enjoy our harvest."

Smith thanks her as he hooks his arms around both our pumpkins, saving me from the embarrassment of having to attempt to pick mine up again. "Lead the way."

I scan the open tables and settle on two in the back placed side by side and head in their direction, Smith following closely behind. "This good enough for you? I wouldn't want you accusing me of cheating when I win."

Smith scoffs, those sapphire eyes rolling. "I wouldn't dare." He sets my pumpkin down before moving to his own table. "So, what are the ground rules?" He rests both arms on the table drawing my eyes to the broad expanse of his back under his yellow flannel.

"Um," I stutter, trying to focus on anything but him. "First no using the books. We've got to carve entirely by freehand. Fifteen-minute limit, that way it's as fair as possible. Oh, and we have to find an impartial judge."

He nods his head, looking up at me through his lashes. "Sounds fair."

We take our time setting up and adjust the materials to our liking. The knives provided aren't the standard carving tools you get when you buy that cheap book from the store that comes with supplies. These are sturdy enough to not bend when you try to saw through the thick rind or snap in half at the slightest movement. These babies are top-notch.

"Okay, big guy. Ready to lose?" I line up my materials in the order I'll need them and glance over at him.

"Are you ready to lose, Care?" He quirks a dark brow at me, his hair bouncing free on his forehead. I chuckle when he tries and fails, to put it back into place. He never could tame that lone piece.

The timer on my phone is set for fifteen minutes and I wiggle my fingers in anticipation. The one thing Smith and I always managed to do when we were together was have fun.

And since he's come waltzing back into my life this week, the fun I used to have has come back with him.

"Ready." My eyes flick over to his hands, making sure he's not cheating. "Set." My finger poises above the button of my timer. "Go!"

Knives clatter as we both rush to get started, my fingers gripping the handle of the largest knife and quickly working to cut around the stem. I'm completely in the zone, locked in on my design, and hellbent on beating the shit out of Smith.

In no time at all, the guts of the pumpkin glide through my fingers, the slimy texture giving me a ridiculous amount of satisfaction. Next to me, Smith lets out a girlish squeal as he works on pulling the seeds and gristle from his pumpkin, making me giggle—he was always a bit squeamish.

Each scoop hits the trash can with a satisfying plop and I begin scraping the sides clean. I know I'm going to win, but on the off-chance I lose—and I won't—I don't want any wayward guts sticking to my hair.

With time quickly dwindling, I have to pear back on the image in my head, instead focusing on doing better than Smith. I can't help it, my eyes flicker over to where he's working at a frenzied pace, and for a moment we catch each other's eye and he gives a tentative smile, one that steals my breath because it fills a need I didn't know I had. A need to be smiled at by someone I—

Nope. Don't go there. Focus on winning.

Pushing away Smith, his heart-warming smile, and the feelings that stir up in me, I get back to my carving before I accidentally cut myself. Being distracted by mister tall, dark, and handsome is dangerous when dealing with sharp objects.

My carving quickly comes to life, and I manage to do it without slicing my hand open. Worried about time, I glance at the timer. "Two-minute warning," I shout too loud at Smith, who doesn't acknowledge hearing me, instead choosing to work in silence as the time clicks down. Within no time at all, the alarm blares with finality and I back away from the table, looking to Smith to see that he's doing the same. We're both covered in pumpkin to our elbows and red-faced from working so frantically.

"Fifteen minutes seems longer than it is," Smith chuckles as he leans back to examine his handiwork. "I can only hope yours looks as terrible as mine." He smiles a crooked smile and tries to peer over my shoulder at my masterpiece.

"Oh hell no," I reach forward and turn my pumpkin, giving him nothing but the orange rind to look at. "I'm not showing you anything until we've picked our judge." I survey the mess we've made in our rush to finish our pumpkins, our tables littered with guts and shavings. "And looking at the mess we made, we need to clean up first."

Smith relents, his hands up in a sign of surrender before scanning his table and cleaning his mess. I do the same; the large chunks of pumpkin thumping into the designated garbage can separate from the seeds and guts. Once our tables are as clean as when we started, we both pick up our much lighter pumpkins and search for a judge.

People walk by, the afternoon sun struggling to peek out from behind quickly gathering clouds. The cool breeze has picked up since we got here, my ponytail whipping behind me from its force. No one pays us any attention as we scan the crowds. "How about her?" I tilt my head in the direction of the young lady working the pumpkin carving stand. "She looks like she can be impartial."

Smith strolls over to her, setting his pumpkin down away from me and making sure I don't peek. Her wide eyes glance my way and a large smile breaks across her face. Her purple beanie sits atop long black hair streaked with shades of violet. "Oh my gosh, I'd totally love that," she squeals, her energy perking up. She stands and gestures for us to come closer. "I'm ready to judge. Lay 'em on me." Her energetic fingers wave toward her, eager to get started.

Smith looks at me, tilting his head for me to go first. "Oh no," I say. "This whole thing was your idea, big guy, so it's all you." Smith looks down at his pumpkin, a frown pulling at his mouth.

"Well, come on. I haven't got all day." Our judge claps her hands before motioning for Smith to show her what he's got.

Smith sighs. "Fine." He spins the pumpkin in his grasp and it's all I can do to keep my pumpkin from slipping from my arms.

It's terrible. Downright awful.

Smith didn't carve this pumpkin: he butchered it. The poor thing has a face built from a nightmare, and not in a good way. Its eyes are the traditional triangles, but large chunks are gouged out around the edges like Smith couldn't get the triangles to pop free. The nose is placed almost even with the eyes, making it look like it has three eyes instead of two. Its mouth is a gaping hole with what looks to be barely hanging on teeth.

The more I look at it, the harder it is to hold back my laughter. "What did you do to your poor pumpkin?" My shoulders shake with laughter as I struggle to keep hold of the pumpkin in my arms. "Smith, that's terrible."

"It's not that bad." He leans forward in an attempt to view his creation, but his composure fractures. That breathtaking grin spreads out on his face, his blue eyes shining with laughter. "You're right," he manages through his chuckles. "It's terrible." The two of us laugh in unison like we once used to do. "I think it's safe to say you've won," he manages between barks of laughter. "Let's see yours."

Spinning the pumpkin while fighting giggles takes some effort, but somehow I manage it.

"That's the best-carved pumpkin I've ever seen." Our judge whispers as she steps closer to examine my work of art. "You didn't use the book?" I shake my head.

My pumpkin is much more refined than Smith's. Its eyes are delicate swirls that were a pain to cut without breaking bits off. They sucked up most of my time, but I was hellbent on having those swirling orbs. Its triangle nose is perfectly centered if I do say so myself, with a curling smile resting underneath. It's easy to picture this pumpkin outside my coffee shop surrounded by my gold and magenta mums.

"You won for sure." Her purple hair bounces up and down as she nods enthusiastically. She looks at Smith, her eyes apologetic. "Sorry, man, there was no way you could compete with that."

An arrogant smile spreads across my face. "Time to pay up, loser."

Chapter Eight

Smith

No amount of bribing was going to win me this and believe me, I tried. Yeah, I might have been too confident going into this, but winning was never my goal. Getting Cara to relax around me was, and from the way her honey eyes are sparkling now, I think I succeeded.

Polly, our judge, offers to hold on to Cara's pumpkin while I fulfill my part of the bargain. She graciously let me back into the carving pavilion free of charge to cut out a hole for my head.

With a huff, I set down the knife and examine the hole I've made and deem it large enough.

Here goes nothing.

Cara's waiting next to the entrance of the pumpkin carving pavilion bouncing on her heels. When she spots me leaving looking like a kicked puppy, she starts clapping, an ear splitting grin on her face. "This is going to be the best day ever."

"Eat it up while you can, Care. Next time I'll be sure to hone my carving skills before we do this again." I hold the pumpkin up and give it one last look before lifting it over my head to rest on my shoulders.

Cara's hysterical laughter seeps in through the thick hide of the pumpkin. It's an odd feeling. I've wanted to hear her unfettered laughter, but now it's directed *at* me and not *with* me. My hands rest on my hips as I let her ride out her fit of laughter, but the gesture has her bending over, laughing so hard no sound comes out. "Alright." I motion towards myself. "Get it out." Now I find myself laughing along with her, not as hard because being inside a pumpkin isn't as funny as it seems.

"I've got to take a picture of this," she manages as she fishes through the purse hanging by her hip for her phone. "Hold still." Through the terrible eyes of the pumpkin, Cara beams at me. Her eyes are lit with that spark from within, her smile wide on her face, and it takes my breath away. "Okay, one, two, three. Cheese!" I hold my arms wide in pride as she takes a picture to gloat about her victory. "That's perfect," she chuckles.

"Here." I offer, reaching for her. "Let's take one together. That way you can show everyone. I know how much you'll enjoy telling them about your win." She agrees and slides under my outstretched arm. My hand wraps around her shoulder, tucking her closer to me. Her arm reaches across my back in a familiar embrace. She's so close I'm sure she can feel the pounding of my heart in my chest. Due to our height difference, she has to lean in, her perfect cheek almost resting against my chest. I smile wide behind my newfound face happy with my current predicament, no matter how embarrassing.

"Time to pay up, big guy." She pats my chest before stepping from my grasp and tucking her phone away. She flicks her wrist to the fields of pumpkins and storm-dark sky. The crowd has thinned out since we arrived, but families still search the fields for their pumpkins.

Cara follows closely behind me as I carefully wander out to the fields. "I can't see where I'm stepping," I toss over my shoulder. It's true enough, my vision is lacking the bottom portion due to the terrible placement of my pumpkin face.

"You just want me to walk next to you. Not gonna happen."

The ground crunches beneath my feet, pumpkins lining either side as I walk carefully down the manicured rows. People stop and stare. Little children squeal with excitement, pulling their parents in my direction.

"They must think you work here," she says with a lilt of amusement to her tone. "This is even better than I could have imagined."

"Live it up, Cara," I mumble under my breath, the vibration of my voice echoing in the shell of the pumpkin. A young family examines a pumpkin down our row and the mom spots me, a grin sneaking across her face.

"Honey, look," she says to the blonde toddler at her feet. His big green eyes look at me before he takes off, his little feet slipping on the dirt. His mom catches him before he falls, setting him upright and grabbing his hand. "Excuse me," she says as they approach, "would you mind if my son takes a picture with you? He loves jack-o'-lanterns."

Cara chuckles behind me. "He'd love that," she jumps in before I can answer. "Why don't all three of you squeeze in for a family photo? I'd be happy to take it for you."

How did I know she was going to say that?

"The more the merrier," I say as the family gathers around me, the little boy looking over his shoulder at me every chance he gets.

One photo bleeds into another as more people gather around us. Cara's living it up, giggling every time she takes another photo of me surrounded by teenagers or when a little kid knocks on my pumpkin.

The crowd has finally died down, and I turn to Cara. "Has it been long enough?" I ask, desperate. We've been walking around for what feels like an hour. "It's getting hot and stuffy in here. Surely I've fulfilled my part of the bargain."

She rubs her hand along her chin, eyeing me as she sucks her teeth. "I'll admit you did go above and beyond the call of duty. I guess I'll take pity on you."

I breathe a sigh of relief and cradle the heavy pumpkin in my hands before lifting it. Except it doesn't move. "Um, Cara," I say through the rising panic building in my chest. "Care, it's not moving." I try to remove my head to no avail. "I think I'm stuck."

"Don't be a baby," she chides. "Here, let me try." She reaches up, replacing my hands with hers on either side of my pumpkin head and pulls. The hole I deemed large enough to get my head *into* is somehow magically too small to get my head *out* of.

"How is this even possible?" she asks through gritted teeth as she tries and fails to free me of my confines. Cara lets go and leans forward, examining the hole resting on my shoulders, the smell of her perfume wrapping around me, breaking through my panic. "Okay, big guy." She grabs my hand and leads me after her. "I have an idea."

The feeling of her hand holding mine sends a thrill through me. Her hand fits perfectly inside my own and I revel in its embrace as she leads me through the fields, her steps confident and sure. People still glance my way, but thankfully no one stops as she leads me over to a hay bale.

"Wait here," she orders, pushing my shoulder down until I sit on a makeshift chair. "I'll be right back."

With nothing better to do, I watch the sway of her hips through my poor excuse for eyeholes. I find myself tilting my head inside my orange prison trying to follow her movements. Polly smiles broadly at her, but all I can make out are small gestures between the two of them. Bursts of laughter trickle over to where I'm perched, barely audible through the pumpkin. Cara slips from my view momentarily before she comes back into sight, her hand wrapped around a knife.

I'm struck again by her beauty as she carefully carries the knife over to where I'm sitting. My eyes linger on the graceful way she moves, the bounce of her chest with each step, the way her long hair swirls in the breeze.

What did I ever do to deserve this second chance? From where I'm sitting, she's far too good for the likes of me.

"Okay, so don't freak out, but I'm going to cut you free," she says when she gets close enough. "I'll have you know I have impeccable knife skills and that you're in safe hands. We'll get you out of here faster than you can say *Sleepy Hollow*."

Her eyes meet mine through distorted triangles. "I trust you." Simple enough words, but the truth in them rings loud between us. "I always have."

Cara pauses and I watch the pulse in her neck pick up speed. The urge to lean forward and place my lips over the thrumming there is overwhelming. I know she wouldn't want that though, and thankfully, or not-so thankfully, the giant pumpkin on my head stops me from making any move.

"Um, just hold still." I don't move a muscle as she carefully slides the serrated blade into the gap between my neck and shoulder. Very slowly, she starts to work the blade into the pulp of the pumpkin. "How's your article coming?"

The whole reason for me being in this town in the first place has been overshadowed by my need to be near Cara. "I've managed to learn a lot about what draws people here. I can see why you came back. It's a special place." Her sawing slows to a halt, her eyes sliding to mine.

"I didn't want to come back," she whispers so soft it barely reaches my ears. "I wanted to stay with you."

Each word is the twist of a knife, the void in my chest growing larger with each passing second. Without thought, my hands reach out to rest on her hips, needing the contact to ground me. "Then why did you leave, Cara? What did I do wrong? For years I've been wracking my brain to pinpoint what happened—where we went wrong—but I feel just as clueless now as I did six years ago."

Cara shakes her head, her ponytail swishing behind her. She focuses back on the knife, the slow and steady sawing continuing. "I think," she says after several quiet moments, "I can cut a straight line to the mouth and then we can pry it open that way." Her hips rock back and forth with her sawing motion, but I won't dare let go, not when she's letting me hold her in this way.

"Sounds good." My voice is gruff in the hollow of the pumpkin that gets darker the longer I sit, the sun stuck behind dark clouds. She's avoiding my question, but I know pressing her for an answer won't get me anywhere. For six years she's left me in the dark, what's one more day?

"Can you turn your head for me? I don't want to catch your jaw on the knife." I do as I'm told, turning my head to the right. "Almost got it." With a quiet pop, the knife juts through the gaping mouth and I fight the urge to look at her handiwork.

There's a cracking sound as Cara pulls the bottom portion of the mouth away and lifts my prison from my shoulders. "There ya go, free as a bird."

Just as I'm enjoying the fresh air on my now-exposed face, Cara snorts out a laugh. "What is it now?" I ask. Her hands grip my shoulder as she laughs, her hair falling in my face. Having her so close, in my arms, smelling her shampoo feels as close to right as I've been in a long time.

"There's," she huffs, "pumpkin. In your hair." Cara straightens, her hands sliding up my shoulders and into my hair. She giggles as her fingers run through the dark strands, the sensation of having my hair played with drawing my eyes closed. My muscles relax under her touch and I tip my head back. On reflex, I pull Cara closer to me, her breath hitting my face, her mouth inches from mine. Her fingers no longer scrape along my scalp, looking for pieces of pumpkin. Instead, it feels more like a gentle caress. Soft hands glide over my temples, her feather-light touches drawing a moan from deep in my throat.

"Smith," she whispers, her forehead lowering to rest against mine. My eyes slide open meeting with the soft honey-gold of hers. I'm too scared to move, to breathe, as we gaze at one another. My hands travel up her sides, one hand coming to cup her jaw.

"Cara," I whisper back as I pull her lips to mine.

Years. It's been years since I've had her lips on mine and yet it's like no time has passed at all. Kissing Cara is finding a ray of sunshine in a dark room. Every touch is illuminating, leaving a trail of scorching heat in its wake.

Cara leans into me, her hands gripping my neck, her mouth slipping open and deepening the kiss. She's the one in control of this, and I'm not going to stop her. Let her remember what we had together, can still have together if she'd let us.

She pulls back, her breathing ragged. "I—"

The darkening sky opens up, rain pouring down from the heavens. In seconds, it soaks through our clothing. Customers run for shelter wherever they can find it, some families huddling under outstretched jackets.

We both look up to the gray late-afternoon sky, surprised at our unwelcome distraction. "I think we should probably get out of this rain," I say, pushing myself off the hay bale that has become a sponge. I reach for her hand and she takes it letting me guide her towards the exit. "I know a place where we can dry off."

Chapter Nine

Cara

Already soaked to the bone, we take our time heading back to the car. Smith pulls me after him stopping for my masterpiece waiting with Polly before closing us into the shelter of the car.

We kissed. I'm still reeling from that kiss. That perfect, heart-stopping kiss should never have happened, but god I'm glad it did. Alive. That's what happened the moment our lips touched. I remembered what it's like to feel alive. And I crave it. I crave the lightning that floods my veins whenever his hand brushes mine; when his lips meet mine.

How had I forgotten?

"We can stop at the bed and breakfast to dry off since it's on the way. If you're okay with that?"

Rain pounds against the roof of the car, the sound almost deafening. "Sure," I reply, still on cloud nine. It's a miracle I'm even coherent enough to speak.

Smith's hand reaches across the dash, coming to rest on my thigh and goosebumps break out on my skin. A shiver runs down the length of my spine and it has nothing to do with being soaking wet. Smith must have noticed because he reaches for the controls of the dash, turning the heat to blasting.

The downpour has made the roads a maze of potholes, the journey out to the paved road is like riding in a four-wheeler. Every bump and jostle made worse as Smith's hand wanders farther up my thigh with each jolt making concentrating on the road near impossible.

Things between us have gotten even more complicated. The way he keeps asking me why I left has anxiety pooling in my stomach. He deserves to know, I know that much, but I can't even admit to myself why I left.

By the time we pull into the long driveway to The Rosebranch, the rain is nothing more than a drizzle. It's been years since I've been here, but I can't say that it's changed much. Darla comes into the shop from time to time and she's as friendly as ever even if she does scoff anytime she sees the covers of my romance books. Old ladies can be such prudes sometimes.

Smith holds the front door open for me and it's like stepping into a time capsule. I've been in Rose Prairie since I was a pre-teen and whenever family came into town, I would find myself bounding up these creaking stairs. The same pictures line the walls which might have been painted at least once in all the years I've been here. Smith chuckles, his hand resting on my lower back as I point out how little this place has changed.

Our shoes squish with every step and for a moment I worry that we'll ruin the carpet with our soaking wet shoes. I glance over my shoulder to make sure we're not leaving a trail of water in our wake. Darla would throw a fit at me if I did.

"My room's to the left." He points down the hallway at the top of the steps. His hand never leaves my back and I wonder if that kiss has reignited something in him too. I know it has in me. If he were to take his hands off me at this moment, it'd be like sucking the oxygen from the room. I'd cease to exist.

This is what I've been trying to avoid. I started out wanting to keep things professional, and here I am, the one that crossed the line. Yes, he pulled my lips to his, but I had started it.

Truthfully, there wasn't a lot of pumpkin in his hair, but I couldn't stop my hand from sweeping through his hair. It unearthed memories of lying in bed together, his head resting on my chest while I played with the dark strands. Memories I've worked so hard to keep out of my head.

Smith showing up at my literal doorstep has thrown me for a loop.

He stops us in front of a solid wood door, a gold-plated eight nailed in the center. "Ignore the mess," he instructs as he turns the key, the lock clicking open.

Stepping into the room, I can't help but laugh. Clothes hang from the large four-poster bed and notebooks are tossed carelessly on the dresser. The picture of the half-naked man on the cover of our book club pick catches my eye, his dark-rimmed glasses resting beside it. "I guess that's another thing time didn't fix. You always were a mess." Not just a mess, but the messiest person I've ever met. Sure, he looks all put together, but the man is a closet hoarder. Alright, maybe he's not that bad, but he leaves a trail of destruction. I could always pinpoint his location by following the debris left in his wake.

He dodges wayward clothing and steps into the bathroom. "Hey, I'll have you know I know exactly where everything is. It's an organized mess. No." He sticks his head through the door jam pointing a determined finger in my direction. "It's organized chaos."

"Don't kid yourself," I tease, catching the towel he playfully tosses at me as he leaves the bathroom.

Across the room, Smith unceremoniously removes his outer flannel, the fabric clinging to his arms as he struggles to get it off. I watch frozen, the towel pressed tight against my damp neck as the black shirt lifts over his head before landing on the floor with a wet splat.

He did *not* look like this six years ago. He was muscular before, but more lean. Now he's downright built. Chest hair is sprinkled across his sculpted pecs leading down to a dark trail that slips below the waist of his pants.

Long gone is the twenty-two-year-old boy. Before me stands the man.

He seems oblivious to my ogling until I notice the slight smirk on his face. "Okay, big guy, I see what you're doing."

"And what is that?" he asks in mock innocence.

"You're trying to seduce me." I point an accusing finger at him rendered ineffective by the towel clenched in my fist.

"I think you're reading into things," he says with a shake of his head. He flexes his muscles so obviously that I laugh. "If you want, I can find you a shirt to wear. Your sweater is dripping on the floor." Sure enough, there's a growing puddle spreading beneath my feet. The sweater that once clung to my curves has stretched down to my knees from the water weighing it down.

A zipper hums and the floor creaks as I examine my sopping-wet sweater that suddenly feels like it weighs a thousand pounds before dropping the towel to soak up the mess I've made. Movement in front of me makes me glance up only to see Smith's naked chest right in my face.

Oh shit.

I swallow, my throat going dry from the view in front of me. "Thanks," I whisper, my voice strained as I take the shirt dangling in the space between us. His eyes burn down on me. He's standing so close that I can feel the heat coming off his skin.

"Now who is doing the seducing?" He asks, his fingers reaching across the expanse between us to run along the collar of my sweater.

My breath hitches at that simple touch. "I don't know what you're talking about." My tongue darts between my lips as my heart flutters.

Smith shuffles closer, his mouth inches above my own. "You can't look at me like that Care, without me wanting you. Having you stand here, in my room, looking at me with hunger in your eyes is the biggest temptation I've ever had." His other hand slips around my head gently pulling my hair free of its ties until it hangs down my back. "I'm giving you the choice right now, Care. You can take my shirt and leave like you did all those years ago." He slides his hand up my neck to rest on my jaw. "Or, you can stay."

Those three simple words unlock something inside me I didn't know I needed. *I can stay*. All those years ago I felt like I didn't have a choice. But I have one now and there's no question in my mind about the answer.

The shirt he handed me falls to the floor, landing among the towel and scattered clothing. He doesn't move an inch as I lift the soaking hem of the sweater. Smith's eyes widen, his gaze drifting down to watch me as I begin to undress. A small sigh of relief leaves his lips as I pull the sweater over my head and let it fall to the floor.

The second I'm free from the wet confines Smith's mouth is on mine. His lips worship my mouth, this kiss nothing like the one that came before it. Smith unleashes everything to me, bearing his heart and soul in one single act. All the pain, hunger, and most of all love seep into every fiber of my being, taking all he's giving me.

Tears I've been holding at bay for what seems like years begin to stream down my cheeks as our mouths work to mend what had been broken.

What *I* broke.

He pulls back, his sapphire eyes filling with unshed tears, his thumb wiping away my own. A hand slowly glides down my spine, leaving goosebumps in their wake until he lifts me into his arms. I slide my hands into his inky black hair, loving the feel of it running through my fingers and bring my mouth down to his.

He holds me tight against him as he carries me to the large four-poster bed, laying me down softly. Smith moves lower, his lips trailing down my throat, kissing his way down my body. My hands trail down his back and across his broad shoulders. He's the last person who ever saw me like this. The last person whose skin has brushed against mine so intimately.

Living without him, without *us,* has been my own form of torment. What had I done all those years ago?

Smith places soft kisses on my stomach as he moves lower down my body. My heart, once pounding, seems to cease beating as he flicks his blue eyes up my body, connecting with my own before he slides off me.

I sit up, a protest ready to spill from my lips.

He stands, his hands never leaving my legs as they come to a stop at my boots. "Relax," he says softly. "There's too many clothes in the way." Looking down, I see exactly what he means.

We're both shirtless, but my bra is securely fastened around my ample chest. He manages to drag the top of my leggings down to my hips, but I'm still covered.

My eyes glance towards Smith as he unzips one boot, then the other. He's hard through the denim of his pants and anticipation gathers in my belly. Looking to help him out, I quickly reach behind me to unclasp my bra and toss it to the side. When I look back, Smith's movement has frozen, his eyes scorching as he takes in my naked breast.

They always were his favorite.

I lay my back flat on the mattress gliding my hands along my skin and sliding them into my damp hair. "Are you just going to stare, or are you going to get me naked?"

Smiths Adam's Apple bobs before he picks up where he left off, tossing my boots behind him. They hit the dresser with a smack making me chuckle. "It's been six fucking years," he mutters with a scowl. "I'm sure as hell going to get you naked, Care. Believe me." With one fluid tug, he manages to free my leggings, dropping them to the floor, his gaze hungry.

"Now you," I order, looking pointedly at the straining zipper of pants. I playfully bite my lip and he chuckles, shaking his head. The way his muscles bunch together as he unbuttons his jeans so distracting that I don't notice he's finally standing naked before me.

Smith wastes no time lifting my left foot to his mouth picking up where he left off, kissing his way up my thigh. His eyes never break contact with mine, the heat and longing in them clear. The higher he kisses the more difficult it is to not break his gaze, to never lose focus of the look in his eyes as he watches me.

When he pauses just before the juncture of my thighs, I break. Shivers of pure anticipation are too much and my eyes squeeze closed waiting for the heat of his mouth. "Cara," he soothes, halting his ascent. "Look at me. I need to see your eyes." It takes more effort than I care to admit to meet his gaze, but when I do, he looks at me so tenderly. "I've missed you," he breathes right before he puts his mouth on me, his eyes wide open.

A rush of breath leaves my body, a low moan going with it. My eyes roll into the back of my skull from the simple tease of his tongue. Pleasure I've long since forgotten builds within me, a damn waiting to burst.

Smith takes his time as he devours me, not stopping to remind me to open my eyes. Dark stands of his hair slip through my fingers as our free hands clasp together. Locked together in this sensual embrace, my body lets go. Tears glide free, my head thrown back as I whimper and thrash in the sheets surrounding me. Smith gently works his tongue over me in featherlight touches as I come undone, our hands welded together.

When my body calms its trembling, Smith gently slides up my body, his lips trailing ever so smoothly along my skin. My hand is still locked in his hair, not quite able to loosen my grip. I pull his mouth to mine. I once thought it impossible to have his lips on mine, so I memorize him, store his taste, his smell, the feel of his skin on mine, the feeling of his weight pushing me into the mattress. All of it.

My legs spread wide as he rests his hips against my own. Outside, the rain hits the windows with a gentle patter like our own personal soundtrack. Smith breaks our kiss, both of our chests heaving. His large hand slips into my hair, his gaze searching for something in mine. I push all the emotions billowing out of me toward him, willing him to feel it. To act on it.

He hums low, pressing his lips against mine once more, his forehead resting against mine as we sit nose to nose.

He says my name like a prayer as he pushes into my welcoming body. For the first time, his eyes flutter closed as he sits himself deep within me, both of us moaning in unison. My eyes are locked on his face and the look of pure awe resting there. I brush back that stubborn strand of inky hair out of his forehead and his eyes flicker open.

"I've missed you too," I breathe as I hold his head in my hands. My head lifts off the mattress as I kiss him slowly, our tongues teasing and exploring. Still locked in our kiss, Smith starts to move in long, smooth strokes.

Our hips move as one, neither of us in a rush. This isn't the time for a frantic coupling lost in everything except for our own pleasure. We make love with each other, every touch and caress aimed to heal the hurt my decisions brought us. Smith presses kisses to my neck, each kiss a unique form of worship.

The pleasure builds in slow increments, each stroke feeding the flames of my desire for him. Smith lets out a groan as he begins to lose control, his movements becoming faster, and deeper.

Now I'm the one dragging his face to mine. Our foreheads rest together, our breaths intertwine, his sapphire eyes filled with desire. My pleasure overtakes me, my orgasm dragging him along with me. Neither one of us loses focus of the other as we find our release with one another. Slowly finding our way back to each other.

Chapter Ten

Smith

It was torture dragging myself out of bed. Especially with Cara still wrapped in blankets and sleeping peacefully. But I have a plan.

We slept through dinner and Darla hadn't batted an eye when I came downstairs barefoot and mussed. She found everything I asked for and I got to work.

I know what happened today is just the first step, the first leap back to what we were. Cara's holding something back, something about what caused her to leave me, to send us both down a long road of heartache. She's never been one to face something head-on, but I need to know. If I don't, I'm not sure how to fully mend the black hole that has started to close since coming to this town.

The door to my room creaks open ever so slightly, but Cara doesn't stir. Even when I slide under the covers and press my body to hers, she stays asleep. I nuzzle my nose into her now dry hair planting kisses along her silky-smooth skin. She lets out a groan, her hand coming up to my shoulder smacking me with a weak swat.

"I was sleeping," she complains in a raspy voice.

I kiss her neck again. "I know. But I have something for us. Get up." She groans pitifully as she rolls over, her hands rising above her head as she stretches. Even like this, all sleep rumpled and stretching, she's the most beautiful woman I've ever seen.

Unable to help myself, I lean down and plant a sweet kiss on her lips before pulling myself away and off the bed. "C'mon sleepy head." For good measure, I smack her delicious ass and am rewarded with a playful squeal.

Cara grumbles under her breath as she crawls out of my bed shooting me dirty looks. She doesn't complain when I toss her one of my T-shirts and a pair of sweatpants. Both will be too big on her but our clothing isn't dry yet. As she slept I wrung out the water that I could and hung them up to dry.

She asks where we're going as she dresses and scoffs when I don't answer. I simply smile and grab several blankets and wait for her by the door. She flips her now dry long dark hair, her earrings glimmering in the lamplight as she stops in front of me and takes the blanket I offer.

Her eyes widen as I lead us out into the hallway. "Smith," she whispers. "What are we doing? People will see us." I slide my arm across her shoulders pulling her against my side.

"Don't worry, Care. We'll be fine." She leans into me as I kiss her head and breathe in the scent of her hair. "I think you'll like it."

Cara's eyes dance in every direction as I guide her down the stairs and out the side door. The crisp, chilly air smells faintly of leaves, our breaths leaving a trail of steam as we walk down the steps and onto the gravel walkway. The rain stopped sometime while we slept, leaving its wet sheen to dance in the starlight.

Firelight blinks in the distance and Cara gasps. The smile she gives me makes my heart stop, so breathtakingly beautiful. "What did you do?"

"A little bit of this, a little bit of that. I thought you'd enjoy having dinner with me." I shrug, smiling down at her. I spot

Hank the closer we get a give a wave of thanks for watching over the firepit while I woke up sleeping beauty. He gives a curt nod before disappearing into the trees, presumably heading back to the house.

The gravel walkway spills out into a wide circle, a blazing fire roaring in the center. Four Adirondack chairs are spaced around the pit, two of them scrubbed dry for us. There's a low table settled between them, an array of food waiting to be eaten.

Cara's stomach lets out an angry rumble at the sight of the food and I pull her close to me as we laugh. "I guess I am hungry," she admits sheepishly.

I make sure she's settled, tucked carefully into the chair with her blanket blocking her from the cold. Her smile is carefree and unguarded as we eat in the firelight.

This is the side of her I've been missing. She talks openly about her life in Rose Prairie, her friends, and her business. In the course of an afternoon, everything shifted.

The soft glow of the firelight reflects off her dark hair, now shimmering with flecks of red and gold usually hidden in the light of day. Each laugh, every smile, works to ease the hole she left.

She humors my questions, playfully teasing me about my inquisitive nature. In return, she peppers me with questions about my life back in the city. The longer we talk in the dim firelight, the more this whole thing feels like a dream. Was it only a few days ago when our lives collided for the second time?

Hours pass as we find each other again.

We're both different and yet the same. What we had in the past clicks together in the present, every piece of the puzzle fitting perfectly. *Except one...*

The crackling fire draws my gaze, and I lean forward resting my elbows on my knees. Hypnotizing flames lock me into their dance, my mind focusing on the one thing that doesn't make sense: why she had left me in the first place.

Cara must sense my shift in focus because she leans into her chair and sighs, her hands clasped around the warm mug of hot chocolate. "This was a good idea. Well done, Smith." She's folded her legs on the seat, the blanket draped over her. She looks so fucking perfect sitting in front of me. So relaxed as she tilts her head back to look at the star-flecked sky.

I hum in response, turning back to the flames and sucking in a steadying breath. Because I know the question I'm about to ask could shatter this illusion of perfection. Ruin the work it's taken to get us to this point. The point where the woman I'm in love with, have been in love with, could tuck tail and run. Run away from me, away from everything we could be. My eyes slide closed, gathering this moment in my memory, of how we are right now.

Her quiet voice cuts through the stillness. "What are you thinking about? You look like you have the weight of the world on your shoulders." The fire lets out a loud pop, the embers catching in the breeze.

"I'm not sure you want to know," I admit, letting out a sigh. She waits patiently as I gather the strength to ask the question that's been burning in me for years. Emotion stings my eyes, my throat clearing on impulse. "Why did you leave?" My voice breaks on the question, overcome with emotion. Tears fill my eyes and I look at Cara. "I don't understand what happened, what I did to have you leave me without a trace. I looked for you, you know. Your apartment, friend's houses, places we hung out at. I can't figure out why."

Cara freezes, her eyes welling with tears. She swallows, those perfect lips parting slightly before closing again. It's like she's on the verge of telling me what happened before shutting down again. Her face, like mine, is twisted with grief.

"Please," I beg.

As if in a daze, Cara sets her mug on the table between our two chairs, the blanket wrapped around her shoulders slipping down to her waist. She rolls her shoulders giving me a hint about the emotions rolling through her. "Smith," she starts, sucking in a deep breath and letting it out slowly. "I can't give you an ans—"

"Bullshit," I hiss. "You know exactly why you left." Anger and hurt simmer underneath my skin. "I love you and you can't even tell me the truth." My head shakes in disbelief, my hair scraping against my forehead with the movement.

Tears stream freely down her face as she stands, gathering the blanket around her. "I can't do this. I need to go."

"Right," I murmur, linking my hands together. "Go and do what you do best. Run off and take my heart with you."

Her face scrunches as tears drip down her chin and onto my shirt. She takes off at a quick pace, running away from me.

Again.

I don't watch her leave because I fear the sight of her back shrinking into the darkness would be my undoing. I deserve to have an answer, to have closure on what happened six years ago.

We both deserve that, because how else can we move on? How else can we grow?

Her footsteps have faded, but the sound of her boots on the gravel walkway lingers in my ears long after she's gone. The slowly dying fire is my only companion in the dark, cool night. I can't bring myself to leave this spot, to push myself out of this seat and trudge up the stairs to the room where we slept only hours ago. To the room where she welcomed me into her body and back into her heart.

A fall mist settles around me, the embers of the dying fire winking out as the sun starts to rise. My hands have long since gone numb, a twin to my numb heart. One day slips into another and the only thing I know for sure is that today I will leave Rose Prairie and the woman I love behind.

Chapter Eleven

Cara

All morning the town square has been a flurry of activity. The Fall Festival begins this evening and will last through the weekend, and from what my customers are saying, they are thrilled about it.

Me? I'm exhausted.

Yesterday was a complete rollercoaster of emotions and I'm still trying to figure out how I feel about it all. I've barely said a word since opening the shop and thankfully Jessie hasn't commented on my robotic state. I plan to keep my head down and try to not think because if I do, I'll spiral.

I spent most of the night lying in bed crying my eyes out. Large bags rest under my eyes, my skin pale and lifeless. My dark hair looks stringy and dull, which is perfect because that's exactly how I'm feeling right now.

That feeling of being alive has been smothered by reality.

The coffee shop is full of visitors and newcomers in town for our special event. Business is booming actually. Unfortunately, I can't feel happy or excited about it either.

Smith has taken up so much space in my heart and in my head that the absence of him, the idea of him being out of my life again, is painful. Was it a mistake to let him back into my life? Is this pain worth it?

Work fills any more contemplation over Smith and this pain in my heart. Time moves quickly as Jessie and I do our best to keep up with the growing line. When backup arrives, we both breathe a sigh of relief. Eileen, Jessie, and I are a well-greased machine, getting orders to our customers quickly. As the line dies down, I let Jessie and Eileen take over orders as I make my rounds throughout the shop.

People happily drink their beverages and walk around the bookstore looking at all it has to offer. Some stop me to chat but the smile plastered on my face doesn't meet my tired, weary eyes. I notice that some customers even carry books around as they look and a tiny spark of joy lights up in my chest before it's smothered once more.

Out the front windows, I spot Sammie and Levi working hard on the final touches of the festival. Sammie points to something, directing Levi as he carries bales of hay. She flails her arms wildly, her hair blowing in the breeze. Levi takes it all in stride, a cheeky grin on his cheeks as he does what he's told. Watching the two of them work side by side, teasing and playful, reminding me of Smith.

Thinking the two of them might need a caffeine pick-me-up, I slide behind the counter and work around Eileen and Jessie. It doesn't take long before I push through the glass door of Tall, Dark, and Coffee and into the cool fall air. I try not to glance down at the golden yellow and burgundy mums and my carved pumpkin sitting with them.

It's a beautiful fall day. The sun shines through the yellow, orange, and brown leaves making the trees look like they're glowing from within. The whole town square has been blocked off from traffic, the streets surrounding the square filling with booths as people work to ready themselves for tonight.

My feet crunch on fallen leaves as I come to a stop next to Sammie. "Long time, no see," I say, holding out her coffee.

Her eyes widen as she spots what I offer, gratefully taking it. "Oh my god, thank you. You're truly the best." She takes a sip and closes her eyes, humming appreciatively.

"How's everything going out here?" Levi unloads another hay bale from his truck, placing it next to the one Sammie points at.

"We're down to the final touches. I keep telling myself that next year things won't be as crazy because we'll already have everything made and figured out, but it's still stressful."

"At least you didn't get trapped in a glowing ornament," I tease with an elbow nudge. Sammie snorts, her shoulders lifting in acceptance. Her fiasco last Christmas is one of my favorite stories. "It looks good though. I think everyone's going to have a blast this weekend."

"Thanks. I wouldn't have been able to do it without my partner in crime." Sammie's voice gradually grows louder, her words traveling not so subtly to Levi where he tosses the last bale of hay onto the pile.

"Partner in crime is better than an assistant." Levi wipes the sweat off his brow and I hold out the warm coffee to my friend. He offers thanks and takes a sip. His eyebrows scrunch together as he looks at me. "You doing okay, Cara?" Levi has known me for most of my life and since we grew up together, he's able to see through whatever bullshit facade I put on.

Sammie's head whips to me, her green eyes wide and full of concern. "He's right." She looks at me like she's never seen me before, no doubt noticing the dark bags under my eyes. "What's going on?" Immediately Sammie goes from event coordinator to caring friend. A warm hand rests on my shoulder and that soothing touch breaks the dam I've placed on my emotions. I turn away from her, trying to block out the embarrassment of crying in public.

Her arms wrap around my shoulder, guiding me past Levi to the discarded hay bales. "It's stupid," I scoff, angrily swiping at wayward tears. "It's about Smith. Old history was dragged back up yesterday and now my feelings are going haywire." I sniffle and look up at the light blue sky, willing the tears to dry up.

Sammie rubs a hand down my back. I called her the night Smith came into town and filled her in on the situation, so thankfully she doesn't make me go into detail. "Do you want to talk about it?" For some reason, this question makes me pause.

Do I want to talk about it?

Half of me thinks, fuck it, talk it out and move on with life. But the other half? The other half is a giant flashing neon sign with the word no blinking rhythmically. I'm not even sure *I* know what to talk about. Smith? My feelings? Why I left? All those questions seem to swirl together in my mind creating a dark whirlpool that leads down into the unknown.

"I think," I stutter, letting out a long breath. "I think I need to figure it out for myself." Levi starts pounding a rubber mallet on a giant wooden pumpkin across the square drawing both of our attention. The hum of volunteers working to get everything set up for tonight seems to grow louder, the quiet bubble around us popping. Sammie's hand stops moving in comforting strokes down my back and I chuckle. "You're dying to get over there, aren't you?"

She rolls her eyes, but we both know the truth—she's a workaholic, especially when she has a project like this to focus on. We sit together on our makeshift bench for several more minutes, never once bringing up the fact that I'm currently an emotional wreck. We part with a quick hug before she jogs over to Levi and picks up the nail gun.

The crowd at the coffee shop has slowed down, both Eileen and Jessie assure me that they don't need my help and can run the front of the shop.

Numbers, figures, and spreadsheets engulf me in their snare as I work on the financial side of owning a small business. My office is small, just large enough for a desk and some nice but functional shelving. The dull red brick becomes my cocoon from the outside world where everything but business fades into the background. Even my thoughts about Smith sink into the back of my mind, the emotions no longer on the forefront, but still there nonetheless. Hours seem to pass in minutes as I bury myself in long-overdue work. At some point, one of the girls brought me a sandwich to keep me from starving.

A gentle knock raps on the door, pulling me out of the numbers and back into reality. "Cara," my office door creeps open and Jessie pops her head in. "Hey, sorry to interrupt," her face forms a nervous grimace.

"You're not interrupting," I assure her, rubbing my weary eyes. "How's everything going?"

Jessie opens the door even more, keeping her hand on the knob. "I was just letting you know the festival has started, so Eileen and I have closed down the shop." The day has flown by and if I listen hard enough, soft music from the festival leaks in through the wall.

"You guys are the best. Thank you." The leather chair squeaks against my back as I let myself relax into it.

"Will you be going to the festival?" Her question is innocent enough, but Smith's face flashes in my mind.

He's going to be there. And then he's gone.

"Um, for a bit."

"Well, I'll see you there." She gives a quick wave before ducking out the door, closing it gently behind her.

I take my time shutting things down doing my best to avoid running into Smith. The Fall Festival has been an exciting event for months, and now that it's finally here, I'm dreading going.

And it's all because I can't be honest with myself. Honest with him.

The orange glow of an autumn sunset filters in through the windows coating everything in its coral and marigold rays. Beyond them, a bustle of people floods the town square, all with smiles on their faces. Little children walk around with their faces painted, couples share pumpkin pie slices, and buy little knick-knacks from booths. Families gather together to take pictures in front of the giant display of pumpkins that Levi and Sammie made, the towering wooden pumpkin almost as tall as the gazebo, with real pumpkins sitting on wide ledges, the changing leaves of the trees acting as a backdrop.

Yet here I stand, looking through the window, unable to bring myself to go beyond these walls. The visual I've painted in my head is a vicious sort of irony. Hasn't Smith been the one I've locked away all these years, kept inside a small box, shut in behind walls in my mind? Isn't he the one who's been standing at the window to my heart and begging for me to let him back in?

Memories from six years ago mix with new memories from this week as I stand and look out at the festival. Me sitting on his couch reading a book while he worked on an article, us driving around the lake with the windows down and music blaring, Smith coming home to find me in his bed, and the wicked grin he would get at the sight. Nothing about our time together was bad or full of problems. We were completely in love.

I'm the problem.

Darkness has settled, the sun's rays quietly dipping below the horizon. Lamplights and perfectly placed lanterns illuminate the square as people continue to enjoy the first night of activities.

I draw a deep, reassuring breath before letting it out through puffed cheeks.

No more running.

Once outside, the full effect of the festival settles in. Music drifts through speakers set up strategically throughout the square. Food vendors are set up in the blocked-off streets, the smell of delicious food wafting by in the breeze. Scarlet, who is working at the Mama's Cakes table selling pies and sweets, offers a kind smile and waves. I give her one back but don't stop to talk. There's a sense of urgency pounding in my head—*I need to talk to Smith*.

For such a small place, it's truly impressive how much Sammie and Levi were able to fit into the square. Not to mention that trying to find one person in this crowd is like trying to find a needle in a haystack. People are packed onto the grassy area, the gazebo, and any open space available. The amount of squeezing between bodies is threatening to make me claustrophobic. I finally find a break in the crowd and take a relaxing breath in an attempt to orient myself.

"Oh, Miss Moore. Just the person I was looking for." Lori Haverford crosses the small space over to me, a delighted smile on her face. "I'm just so glad I found you. These gatherings are wonderful, aren't they?" She swats her hand through the air dismissively. "Anyway, I've been wanting to thank you for introducing me to Matthew. He's such a handsome and kind young man. Spoke very highly of you, I must say. But how thrilling is it that he's writing about our town? You know, I knew that hiring Miss Williams was a good idea."

Thankfully, my scoff goes unnoticed as she drones on. Sammie was public enemy number one for Mrs. Haverford since the day she was hired. She even tried to get her fired.

"But having that young man come here is such a gift. It's a shame he had to leave so quickly. He even let me walk him to his car. Such a gentleman."

"Wait," I stammer. "He's left already?" He's not supposed to leave until tomorrow morning. Dread at the thought of never seeing him again settles into my stomach.

Lori nods her head, her eyes sad. "Not five minutes ago. He seemed a little downcast if you ask me. Such a handsome man shouldn't be so sad," she tsks.

A tall man with a white handlebar mustache steps behind her, his deep voice rumbling as he says her name. She turns sharply on her heels, her mouth falling open.

I don't bother to excuse myself from the conversation before pushing my way back into the crowd. The dawning realization that he could leave Rose Prairie, and me, behind sends me into a panic. My stubborn self has waited too long to be honest, and now it might be too late.

All niceties gone, I push my way clear of the crowd, ignoring all the complaints aimed my way. My feet hit the pavement in quick slaps. I have to walk a block to get to my car since I was unable to park off the main street, and I waste no time rounding the side street to my car. The keys jingle in my hands as I fumble for the fob to unlock my car.

Surely he hasn't gotten too far, right? I can still catch him.

With a wish and a prayer, I slam my foot down on the gas, hoping like hell the cops are all busy at the festival. The engine roars to life as I speed out of town, unwilling to let Smith leave without knowing the truth—the same truth I only just allowed myself to realize.

The town passes in the window in a blur, my foot not once letting off the pedal. Finally, a sleek sedan comes into focus in front of me and all I can think is that it *has* to be him. I need it to be him.

Urging my car faster, I ease into the opposite lane on the two-lane highway, ignoring the no-passing signs. I glance through the passenger side window to look at the driver, but it's too dark to see who's behind the wheel. Cutting in front of the car, I start to slow down, hoping he's not reckless like me, and breaks the no-passing rule. I tap the brakes, the red light illuminating the cab of the car behind me just enough to make out the familiar silhouette of Smith.

Honking my horn I signal to pull over, my hand pointing to the side in emphasis. Gravel and grass crunch beneath my wheels and as soon as I come to a stop, I fling the door open.

"What the hell is wrong with you?" Smith yells, his door slamming shut behind him. "You could've gotten hurt." He runs his hand through his dark hair, concern etched on his face.

"I was scared," I spit out in a rush. "I left because I was scared of what I felt for you. I was young, I'd never been out on my own before, and you came crashing into my life. Here I was, a twenty-one-year-old girl who had goals and dreams, but when I met you none of it mattered. All that mattered was the smiles you gave me, your sweet touches. Your love. I was scared," I say again. "I was scared of what I felt—what I *still* feel for you." Smith doesn't retreat as I reach my hand through the space between us to rest on his chest. "I was scared," I say, as I let out a broken sob.

"What are you saying?" he asks, his voice desperate. His hand tips my chin up, his blue eyes soft. Tears run down my face and he carefully wipes them away.

"I'm saying I love you. I've always loved you. Never stopped loving you. I convinced myself that the best thing to do was to leave. Walk out your door and focus on myself—a clean break. Because I couldn't do it with you looking at me. I wouldn't have been able to turn around and walk out. I wasn't strong enough. I think a part of me always knew I was making a mistake, and we've both paid the price for it."

Smith swallows hard, tears threatening to spill from his eyes. "Say it again."

My hands slide up his strong chest to cup his jaw. "I love you," I breathe. "I've always loved you. Never stopped."

A wistful smile touches his mouth before he kisses me. He pours all his love into this one, world-stopping, all-encompassing kiss. He pulls me closer to him, deepening the kiss until I'm completely wrapped up in his embrace.

Smith kisses me like I'm the answer to all his prayers, and maybe I am because the man in my arms is mine.

When he pulls back, we're both breathless. Smith runs his hands along my jaw, brushing strands of hair out of my face. "I love you." Three simple words uttered on a dark road never sounded so sweet.

"The Best Town In the World"

The Daily Click
Written by Matthew Smith

A picturesque drive on a two-lane highway will lead you straight to what some call the best town you'll ever step foot in.

Rose Prairie, a mere three-hour drive from the suburbs, is the town movies are modeled after. It's a town that moves at its own pace. People wander down the sidewalks on cold, fall mornings, stopping to greet their neighbors by name before heading into one of the locally owned shops that ring the square.

The town of Rose Prairie has recently been making waves, its name reaching far and wide. For over a century, their Christmas Spectacular every Christmas Eve is the town's claim to fame. People from all over flock to the small town to see the magic of Christmas when the lights click on.

The person who makes this dream come true? Miss Samantha Williams of Chicago was hired as the new event coordinator last Christmas. She partnered with a local carpenter, Levi Ross, to create new attractions for the special event. Some say that Miss Williams and all of her hard work have boosted the town's morale. According to lifelong resident Lori Haverford, "Miss Williams and her creativity have been a wonderful presence in our town. Since she's taken over as the event coordinator, Rose Prairie is the best it's ever been."

If you ask Miss Williams about her work, she'll smile gratefully but give credit back to the town and its people. "There's nothing special about me. It's the town, the heart of the people, that makes everything worthwhile."

Not only is Rose Prairie drawing people in for their Christmas Spectacular, but Miss Williams, with the help of Mr. Ross, has created events that draw people in for every season. The First Annual Valentine's Day Love Festival was held this February, helping boost small businesses.

Barbara Clement, co-owner of Mama's Cakes Bakery, had this to say: "She [Miss Williams] does a great job with community outreach. She got in contact with Rosewood College and got their Art Department to create some custom pieces. Local businesses set up booths and open their stores to different activities. It's really helped keep business afloat after the busy holiday season."

The most recent business-boosting event is the town's first Fall Festival. This three-day event is the first of its kind for the small town to put on, and it did not disappoint. Families of all ages wander around the bustling town square. Businesses set up tables on the closed-off streets offering everything from smoked BBQ to gourmet sandwiches and sweet desserts. Children run around with faces painted like lions and tigers, and the occasional fairy. One of Miss Williams and Mr. Ross' newest creations is a forty-foot-tall wooden pumpkin that was the hit of the festival. Visitors stood in wonder in front of the massive structure that houses live pumpkins resting on shelves, each family crowding together to get photos taken by Rosewood College photography students.

Still not convinced Rose Prairies is all it's cracked up to be? Cheryl and Hugh Rogers were married fifteen years ago at The

Lookout, the town's namesake. The Lookout is a field of prairie roses that bloom each spring and summer. "We try to come here once a year. Try to relieve the day and wander through the town. It holds a special place in our hearts."

As for this journalist, like many who visit here, I plan to one day make this special town my home.

Epilogue

Smith

The Lookout is even more stunning than I imagined.

Fall slipped into winter and before we knew it, the warmth of spring and summer arrived. Wildflowers bloom in all their glorious wonder, vibrant yellows, purples, blues, and pinks are sprinkled along the wide valley. The stone ledge that overlooks the entire valley itself is picturesque, its overhang jutting out so far over the valley that it's like you're flying.

"This will be perfect." If I breathe deeply, the sweet smell of the flowers below would engulf me.

Hank clasps me on the shoulder, his grip firm and reassuring. "I figured it would be," he says softly. Hank and Darla quickly became some of my favorite people in Rose Prairie and their help has been instrumental in me being able to pull this off.

Being in a long-distance relationship has its hardships, sure, but the past seven months have been the best of my life. My weekends are spent traveling back and forth, but the drive is easy considering the woman who waits for me at the end of it.

Hank drives us back to the Rosebud and sends me off with a firm handshake.

The drive into town is now second nature, and I raise my hand in greeting as I pass pedestrians, something I never would've thought to do before. Cara has no idea I'm in town and the thought of her reaction seeing me here brings a smile to my face.

The bell dings as I step into the coffee shop, the smell of coffee surrounding me. I breathe in the rich aroma.

Eileen is working behind the counter, and she smiles in surprise. "Hey. I didn't think you were going to be here this weekend."

"That's what Cara thinks," I say with a wink. "Where is your beautiful boss, anyway?" I scan the storefront and don't spot her hidden among the rows of bookshelves.

Eileen throws her thumb over her shoulder. "In her office." I tap the counter and give her a quick thanks as I head down the hallway.

As usual, she's tucked behind her desk, her nose to the screen as she types away on a calculator. Her long hair is down today, a rare occasion, which is going to be perfect for pictures. So engrossed in her task, Cara doesn't notice me, so I take the time to admire her. Her lips are parted slightly, and her eyebrows furrowed in concentration. How she manages to sit like that for hours on end, I'll never know. But it might explain why she's always rolling her shoulders, something she still hasn't managed to figure out she does.

We've gone through so much, and worked through so much, that our relationship today is leaps and bounds compared to what it was six years ago. No more running or hiding feelings. Well, I'm currently hiding something, but she'll find out soon enough.

Something alerts her to my presence and she jumps in her seat, her hand flying over her heart as she gasps in shock. "You asshole! You scared me." Her words lack anger, a smile spreading across her mouth as she runs toward me and jumps into my arms. Her black skirt slips up her thighs as she hooks her legs around my waist. "I didn't know you would be here today."

Her hair smells fruity from her shampoo and I breathe her in, planting a kiss on her neck. Cara pulls back, her hands running through my hair as she brings her mouth to mine. God, I hope I never get used to her kisses. Let every single one of them be as exciting as the first.

I gently set Cara back on her feet, my hands smoothing the hair from her face. "I missed you. Plus, I have a surprise."

A dark eyebrow rises. "Should I be scared?"

"Maybe just a little," I tease, my thumb and finger coming close together. "Can I pull you away from your work for the rest of the day?" Cara looks over to her desk, her tempting lips puckering in thought.

"Absolutely. My eyes are getting tired, anyway." She steps out of my embrace, shutting down the computer and tidying her desk.

"I must have perfect timing." My hand slips into my pocket and pulls out a blindfold. "Because I need you to wear this."

She sighs and turns around so I can tie the blindfold. "You better not be doing anything stupid, big guy. I'll have you know that I'm well prepared to kick your ass in whatever shenanigans you have planned."

"Oh, I don't doubt it," I laugh. "But I think you'll like this." Carefully I lead a blinded Cara down the hallway, out the door, and into the car.

The entire way to The Lookout, Cara guesses at what we're doing, each one more ridiculous than the last.

"Nope," I say again. "You're not even close, Care." The car comes to a stop in the empty dirt parking lot of The Lookout. "Plus, we're here, so you might as well stop trying." Cara throws her hands up, her mouth pouting adorably.

"Are you sure I didn't get anything right?" She asks as I open her door.

"Give me a minute and you'll see." Grabbing her hands, I help her out of her seat and lead her to the edge of The Lookout. I spot the photographers I hired, one out in the field, the other ten feet away, her hand poised on the shutter.

Keeping her hand in mine, I gently lower myself onto one knee and suck in a steadying breath. "Okay. Take your blindfold off."

"Finally," she scoffs, tugging the blindfold roughly off her face. Hair tangles in her face and she hurriedly swipes them away before she takes in the scene around her. The rapid clicks of the camera catch every minute expression on her lovely face. Her hand clasps over her open mouth, her honey eyes wide and brimming with tears.

"Cara," I breathe. "From the day I met you, I knew you were the only woman for me. Even when we were apart, there's been no doubt that you're mine. You fill the void in my heart. You're the warmth in my chest, the brightest spot in my life. Will you make me the luckiest man in the world and marry me?"

Tears stream down both our faces as she nods her head. "Of course, I'll marry you."

Thanks For Reading

T hank you for reading *It Had To Be You*!
    When I was first creating the small fictional town of Rose Prairie, all these possible storylines started floating through my head and Cara's was one of the first. I knew she would have a coffee shop and romance bookstore and that someone could come into town and flip her world upside down. Through Cara, I was able to bring my own dream of owning a bookstore and coffee shop to life.

I hope you enjoyed this fall-filled story and the town of Rose Prairie. There are more fun, heartwarming stories coming to this amazing town and I can't wait for people to enjoy them.

If this is the first of my books that you've read and want to read more, check out the completed Claiming Her Series[1] that follows the Williams siblings. Each book follows a sibling and their love connections.

If you're looking for small-town spicy romantic comedies, check out The Rose Prairie Series[2]. I'm loving this small town and look forward to adding more storylines.

Want a spicy age gap? *Yes, Captain*[3] follows Hannah as she joins the crazy crew on the motor yacht Siren and its new

---

1. https://www.amazon.com/dp/
   B0BJCM3QPR?binding=kindle_edition&ref_=ast_author_bsi

2. https://www.amazon.com/gp/product/
   B0BS273PS2?ref_=dbs_p_pwh_rwt_anx_b_lnk&storeType=ebooks

3. *https://a.co/d/jbq88jy*

captain Anson. What she plans to be a relaxing few weeks working on the yacht turns into a forbidden romance as sparks fly between the captain and stewardess.

If you could, please take a moment to rate and review on Amazon, Goodreads, Instagram, or wherever you post reviews. As an indie author, ratings and reviews are the best way of getting my work out there for other people to read. A little goes a long way!

Don't forget to follow me on Instagram @authorsierrashipley [4] and sign up for my newsletter [5] to get freebies and see more details about my coming books!

Thank you for your support!

Until next time,

Sierra

---

4. https://instagram.com/authorsierrashipley?igshid=YmMyMTA2M2Y=

5. https://mailchi.mp/db7893726a2a/sierra-shipley-newsletter-sign-up-page

About the Author

Sierra Shipley is a born and raised Midwest girl. She spends her days with her lovable rescue pup, Trip, who constantly wants all the cuddles. Her ideal day is spent drinking coffee, reading, and dreaming.

Sierra has always wanted the romance she's read in books. Pair that with an active imagination and a love of creativity, and you get a writer!

Her goal is to create steamy, romantic stories with characters that people can relate to.